Daniel Thompson was born and lives with his fiancée in Bury St Edmunds, has a love of comic books, science fiction, horror and heroic fantasy stories.

This Chained City

Daniel Thompson

This Chained City

Copyright © D a n i e l   T h o m p s o n

The right of Daniel Thompson to be identified as author of this work has been asserted by him in accordance with section 77 and 78 of the Copyright, Designs and Patents Act 1988.

All rights reserved. No part of this publication may be reproduced, stored in a retrieval system, or transmitted in any form or by any means, electronic, mechanical, photocopying, recording, or otherwise, without the prior permission of the publishers.

Any person who commits any unauthorized act in relation to this publication may be liable to criminal prosecution and civil claims for damages.

All characters in this publication are fictitious and any resemblance to real persons, living or dead, is purely coincidental.

A CIP catalogue record for this title is available from the British Library.

ISBN 978 1 84963 212 6

www.austinmacauley.com

First Published (2012)
Austin & Macauley Publishers Ltd.
25 Canada Square
Canary Wharf
London
E14 5LB

Printed & Bound in Great Britain

To my Dad, who always encouraged me, drove me and inspired me.

"You, Halt!!"

The young Constable of the Pelimarian Security Corps ran after the would-be-terrorist. As he sped away the explosive device still in his hand, a featureless black mask sheathed his features.

She fired her weapon; a bolt smashing into the ancient masonry, the bomber turned a corner, behind two connivance shops. Weighed down by twenty pounds of protective armour, as she ran after her prey, her short hair hardly moved in the wind.

The young woman turned the corner to find the alleyway empty.

"Aw, sh–" she exclaimed, just before the terrorist appeared from the darkness behind her and knocked her out.

I

The dark battered form of the Security Corps craft lifted gracefully up into the air, pushing off from the heat-blasted and laser-scarred landing grid.

DuSalle, formerly Constable of Western Quad 207, looked regretfully down through the transport's grit-scarred passenger window, sighing as the green and blue domed agriculturally entrenched buildings came into view below.

The craft turned in the air, enabling him to look out over the factory robots working diligently and methodically churning through the fields of the Western Quads, tossing black dust into the air as they passed.

It had become quite a good home to him.

'Til now, thought DuSalle sombrely. As he shuffled uncomfortably around in the bucket seat of the shuttle, a stilted computerised voice blared over the shuttle's speaker system.

"*Attention! Attention!* All passengers must remain seated during take-off sequence from Western Quad Base two–oh–seven. Flight arrival to Chandler City Eastern Quadrant two–four-two will be approximately one hour. Thank you for your good will and patience."

As the gravity coils gave a slight whine, DuSalle settled himself quickly back as he was pulled deeper into the squashy impact proof seat, the craft shooting forward as the horizontal thrusters fired gutturally into life.

The newly promoted Detective pulled himself forward, pressing his forehead against the heavily armoured Plexiglas to look down as the dusty laser cut streets spread out from the brown and grey clusters of open fields, melding into the scattered black structures of the processing factories and product farms. Their fumes funnelled back into the generator houses. As they were pumped outside the protective domes into the toxic atmosphere of the planet, they sped past under him to catch his final glance.

DuSalle had served a good few years as a Constable on the streets that now being swept away from him.

The Western Quads of Chandler City had been his home since he had left the Security Corps Training School. Now he was reassigned to the Eastern Quads of the grand colonial city. The metropolis was full of mile high structures and floating penthouses, the streets cloaked in darkness while the rooftops were crisped with the ruddy haze of sunlight.

The Eastern Quads housed many of the intergalactic merchant and shipping companies that had sprung up during the arrival of the opulent but feudal empire of the Stellar Sovereignty.

Well before all that, Chandler City had been one of thirty colonial outposts sent out into the depths of space by the former Planetary Unity.

Like the others, this city was built billions of miles away from its launch point. Created by robotic hands, hundreds of domed structures that stretched miles into the atmosphere, generated within pockets of air for the colonists to inhabit, enclosed from the toxic atmosphere of the planet.

Now almost a thousand years later, the city sustained itself with the outer domes hemmed by genetically enhanced forests, a leftover from early unsuccessful terra-forming attempts on the planet's surface for the future needs of the city's people.

Thinking about the Eastern Quads, however, brought back the old thoughts for DuSalle, which had been circling in his head since the message he had received a week before:

Con. R. DuSalle
(Street Section, 23rd Sabre Division, Unit 57),
Due to your action in the field of duty, you have been accordingly promoted to the post of Detective (Third Class) on advice put forward by Quadrant Commander K. Bryst (W.Q. 207). As such you are also reassigned, effective immediately, to Street Section proper to Eastern Quadrant 242 (Com. T. A. Vice, OM)
So ordered by
Chief of Central Quadrant Administration,
H. L. Yameth

Who was he to be partnered with? Would they rank higher than him? What would they expect of him in the Eastern Quads? These along with a thousand similar thoughts, had passed through his head, soon enough he knew these questions would be answered.

Whether he would like them or not was another thing entirely.

DuSalle watched the transition between the Chandler City Quads, with a deep unease in the pit of his stomach as he left the familiar behind, the craft travelled into the connecting tunnels between the massive domes.

The craft passed over industrial buildings, massive right-angled tubing coiling across them like stiffened strike-worms. Their mass of metal girders fell away to smaller private residences intermixed with flyovers and – unders. Roads straightened out and vanished into slim alleyways passing through taller buildings.

Then finally, the craft was in the Eastern Quads, into the grand metropolis. DuSalle sucked in a breath in amazement.

He had seen the metropolis of Chandler City through holograms in his early school training. It was a forest of magnificent mile-high structures of metal, concrete and fibreglass limitlessly stretching up, seeming to cut through the massive domes under which they were housed.

Moving in grid-like formation were lines of civilian traffic, hanging like decorations between the massive structures. Closer to one of the buildings they passed, were tiny winding pedestrian walkways, which may have been dangerous so high up but for the gravity seals on them.

From a distance, DuSalle could never have imagined the vast nature of the city. As he now viewed its depth into shadow and its height into the endless veil-like cloud, which seemed to permeate the peaks of the domes in the lone city of Pelimar.

He was shocked out of his reverie as the transport cut to half speed, jolting him forward.

DuSalle pressed the side of his face against the glass in an effort to see before him.

The transport easily glided its bulk through oncoming traffic, past large graffiti-covered metal struts that steadied the massive formations from quakes.

As they were nearing the edge of what the scientists called the 'Gavin tectonic plate', buildings were lower with more of the heavily fortified anti-shock struts.

Then the craft broke through a cluster of taller buildings, surrounding the Mully reservoir, leading into a metal and concrete carved valley.

Awash with dim sunlight of dawn, here the traverse ways and sky-roads opened up to reveal the impressive hump-shaped tower of the Eastern Quadrant Base Headquarters.

The craft drifted onward, closing on the building, cutting its speed further, beginning its descent.

DuSalle was jolted only lightly this time as Central Air Control took over the piloting of the craft for the landing.

It settled lightly as a leaf onto the blinking red neon landing pad, booster coils retracting as its landing gear unfolded to the ground.

DuSalle disembarked quickly, taking his bundle of belongings from the overhead compartment which contained all his gear from his old locker.

Then moving along the aisle, past other grey and purple garbed officers of the Security Corps, DuSalle stood in front of the pressurised door, waiting for it to open.

The fact that he alone was bound for the Eastern Quads set DuSalle on edge more than it would have in a large crowd.

As the light above pinged to green and the door opened, DuSalle strode purposely forward, through the pressure door and down the metal steps into the early haze, breathing in the burnt air that swelled thickly around him from the shuttle's landing.

DuSalle rolled his shoulders as his tightly fitting uniform was still rather uncomfortable, certainly when compared to his old Patrolmen's basic jumpsuit, of which he missed the comfortable fit. This uniform was more rigid and enclosing.

"Good morning, Detective DuSalle," called a voice. DuSalle turned to owner of the low voice to see a man dressed in the same grey tunic, trousers and high purple collar as himself.

There were subtle differences to their uniforms. This man had a bandolier attached to his Corps utility belt from right hip to left shoulder which had a silver pip of Second Class rank. That meant this grey haired and lined face man was in the Administration Section.

The craft behind DuSalle, as he approached the other officer, lifted off with a brief whine to continue its shuttling duties elsewhere, gifting them with a less turbulent breeze than when it arrived.

As they closed the last few steps, the Admin official smiled, deepening the lines in his wrinkled features.

"Greetings, Detective. My name is Second Official Julian Cartier," said the uniformed man. DuSalle took off his left gauntlet in order to shake the man's hand briefly, while the other officer's large knuckled hands were free of such things.

Cartier gestured for DuSalle to follow him. "Since you're the only one newly assigned here, Chief Vice has asked me to escort you around. Though as you know all Quad Bases are alike, there have been a few modifications. You'll need a new *PummelFist* issued, as procedure of course."

"You mean that my *PummelFist* was deactivated upon my arrival on the transport, Sir?" reeled off DuSalle without thinking.

"Yes, that's right, Detective," said Cartier. "This has rendered it impossible for you to use it on the other passengers or flight staff, as has been known to happen to certain officers, induced by stress or panic during their transition periods." Such was the training that half the time officers spoke with one another they were paraphrasing or directly quoting from the Training School Manuals and Texts.

"Yes, Sir."

"So I have been charged to show you around, before you get 'stuck in' as it were." A grin flashed across his thin features, which were probably used to gravity movement, rather than thrusting dome-ward.

"Thank you Sir. It's a pleasure to be here," said DuSalle, with a tight-lipped smile.

DuSalle's tour guide brought him into the main foyer of the building.

In the centre of the main foyer was a semi-circular desk, raised by several feet to tower over the line of multi fashion-clad citizens, several of whom had arresting officers standing beside them.

Seated at the desk was a tall man with a permanent broody expression of cynical helpfulness set on craggy features, with palms firmly planted on the desk either side of his bulky and imposing frame.

"Sergeant," said Cartier to the Desk Officer, as they bypassed the line. He was leering down his nose at a leather clad, greasy haired man, who stood dumbly cuffed to an officer. He lifted an eyebrow slightly as his gaze moved to them. "This is the new Detective." Cartier pointed to DuSalle, who exchanged a nod with the Officer. "DuSalle is the name."

"I'll punch you in Detective." The Desk Sergeant turned to his console. His left hand seemed bulkier than the other and let out a soft mechanical whirr as he typed in the information.

A small smile flicked across the flint chipped mouth as he manipulated the files.

The Desk Sergeant handed Cartier the neon blue cylindrical info-chip that popped out from under his main console. "Good luck with your new partner, Detective, you'll need it." The Desk Sergeant smirked.

DuSalle frowned confusedly at the man, who had already turned away to the line of twitching first-time snitches and guilty looking good citizens.

"What did he mean by that, Sir?" asked DuSalle, as he was led away by Cartier.

"Doesn't matter, Detective," said DuSalle's guide, dismissively. "When you're sat at that desk, for a sixty-two hour-a-week shift, it tends to make you a little tense. To release that tension you pile it on others."

"We don't all do that," muttered DuSalle darkly, glancing over his shoulder at the Desk Sergeant as he took the details of a citizen who was being carefully subdued by his arresting officer.

"Yes, well. Let's start, shall we?" declared Cartier, with a brisk falsely warming smile as they entered the ascend shaft.

Cartier keyed in his security code. A rigid computerised voice, its tone only mildly different to the shuttle, asked for vocal confirmation and floor, to which Cartier answered "Cartier, Julian G., Second Official of Admin Level eighty-four."

There was a slight jolt as the ascend shaft rose, then an audible ping as the floors were counted off by the computer's monotone voice.

"Like most of the Quadrant Bases, or Quad Bases, as they are commonly known to the populace," said Cartier turning to DuSalle, sounding like an emotionally stilted tourist holo' programme. "It has many different Sections, which you know, of course, Detective. Street, Medical, Tech and so on. We have a new sub-section of Tech, sort of research and development, which was authorised by the Directorate. It was installed here just recently, sort of a test run for the moment. *Special Weapons Tech* is where we shall also collect your *PummelFist.*" Cartier, grimaced slightly, signalling the end of the speech, and continued in his more normal voice. "I believe the new section was invented because of the recent rise in protest riots and violence that have come up in the last few years."

"You mean the Isolationists and the Unionists?"

"That's right," replied Cartier. "The People's Island Movement, the Isolationist Faction, and the Galactic Ascension and Inclusion Association, the Unionist Faction, have been very forthright about the situation between us, the Stellar Sovereignty and the Pastoral Regions, which has led to a few riots and several attempted bombings. Nothing hi-tech, mostly home grown." Cartier looked uncomfortable. DuSalle thought it right for an Admin Officer to be uncomfortable about a situation he probably had no training for, but by the look of Cartier's stocky build, he would have fitted into the Street Section easily. DuSalle wondered idly if he used exercise equipment or the locker room gymnasiums. "Only a few were successful, however." He continued, "They say they have nothing to do with it, contrary to the evidence of a P.I.M. promotional badge which was found on the several of the scenes."

"So they haven't been taken seriously?"

"No, no. Of course not," said Cartier, smiling confidently. "They implied that it's a separate faction, which has been going for the past few months, carrying out these bombings. Precautions have been stepped up since then, as the Isolation Parade is only a few days away."

"It might have something to do with the fall of the crime rate, which I had heard about," said DuSalle, thinking out loud. "There were fewer major crimes going on around the city for the last three months."

"Criminals becoming moralistic anarchists? It's a possibility, I suppose, Detective," said Cartier, though his tone belied the fact he believed it at all.

The shaft doors opened. "Follow me, Detective. I'll introduce you to the Chief of Special Weapons Tech."

* * *

They came into a corridor, moving in between rushing lab-coated people carrying various pieces of equipment or apparatus. A cube shaped cleaner droid, with blinking sensory diodes, moved stoically and methodically, circular mops mopping and waxing the metal plating of the floor, humming and whirring past them.

Cartier led DuSalle to a large blast proof door unlike several others that were lined up either side of it. It covered a big section of wall. 'SWT' etched into the metal surface, with a small plaque declaring '*NO EXPLOSIVE ITEMS TO LEAVE THIS AREA*'.

Shouldn't that be on the other side of the door? thought DuSalle ruefully, though outwardly he did not show any sign that he thought anything of the like.

Cartier entered the security code into the pad set beside the door.

It slid aside. DuSalle winced in anticipation of the expected noise, but the loud scraping he would have expected of a door so heavy looking did not come. Instead came a soft hiss, revealing a loud banging that issued from the inside of the room.

What was inside amazed the newly promoted Detective. It was a hectic hive of explosive activity.

The large room was domed with a high ceiling, allowing a second level to be added to the back of the room. The main floor seemed to be quartered into sections, with various weapons being tested in a small gun range, while in another part at the back were weapons being dissected in gravity clamps.

In that one corner, three lab-coated officers held an assortment of weapons, from a Corps issue horse shoe shaped *PummelFist*, the Security Corps standard sidearm of all Street Section, to a bulky *Slasher* rifle, with stunted barrel, stocked with rubber projectile rounds, which the Municipal Militia and SPUD groups used as their standard weapon, spitting ion charged rounds into the dummy targets suited up in Security Corps street armour.

While in other areas of the room, officers were meddling with various crime fighting and prevention gadgetry, which gave off an assortment of bangs and hisses as they were activated and tested.

"Follow me, Detective," bellowed the Admin officer over the noise of the testing carnage.

Cartier led DuSalle to a far corner, where a man with receding white hair and wearing a grey lab coat over his greasy overalls, was meticulously working over a weapon, which hung in the air in front of him in dismantled parts, which DuSalle could not fully identify.

Cartier called out over the noise. As the man stood with his back to them, DuSalle was surprised for a moment, as the Detective realised that Cartier was not simply shouting out a greeting to the room in general. The Admin Officer called out again as they came closer.

"Hallow!"

The man turned to face them, peering over a pair of half-moon glasses, an unabashed almost innocent smile on his crinkled features.

"Ah, Cartier," he said, in a loud delighted tone. "Nice of you to come down and see how the place is shaping up."

"That's not the only reason, Hallow," said Cartier, moving DuSalle forward like a prized piece of technology for the other to inspect. "This is the new Detective, sent over from the Eastern Quads."

Hallow shook hands with the young Detective, with a half-smile. "It's nice to see a fresh face. What you see here, Detective, is the newest ethic in criminal prevention and eradication, which will advance us into the next century for sure."

"Yes, indeed," agreed Cartier. "You've been working on a few things, I see." He pointed to the pieces of plastic and wiring, which hung in the air behind Hallow.

"Ah, yes," said Hallow, turning to his bench behind him and adjusting the gravity vice, causing the pieces caught in the gravity suspension field to twitch to the right. "As you both know, the *PummelFist* is a weapon that uses laser bolts – charged slits of light to be crude." He pointed to three small tubes amongst the wiring. "The power cell of the weapon is highly radioactive, but this small amount can keep the charge at full for almost a full six weeks, if used in moderation of course." He smiled at them over his shoulder, then looked back at his work. "And with the certain advances we have made, we have been able to tip these 'slits' of light with different properties, such as heat seeking ability and explosive charges – even to a slight degree a ricochet affect – although the tests have been rather random in their directional properties." He grimaced, but then brightened.

"Oh, really?" said Cartier, delightedly interested. DuSalle rolled his eyes internally at the tech officer's improper childish delight, but stepped forward with Cartier. "Very interesting Hallow."

"Very interesting, Sir," said DuSalle, stiffly, hoping Cartier would get the point. He wanted to get 'stuck in' as Cartier had said, as soon as possible, not stand around gabbing.

"Well, anyway, Hallow," said Cartier, seeming to come back to himself, pulling back from inspecting the weapon. "Just thought I'd see what was going on I'm always fascinated by weaponry as you know. But, this young fellow here needs a new *PummelFist*."

"Oh, well, maybe next time I can show you a bit more, Cartier," said Hallow, who seemed genuinely disappointed. "I have a lot of interesting objects you should see. But, like you say, business first. In fact," he brightened, as he twisted a few knobs on gravity vice's control board. "Detective DuSalle can be the first recipient of the *PummelFist* mark 4.7." The pieces flew together, adjusting and fitting to create the thick bulbous handle and hand guard, that also doubled as armoured knuckles, a push thumb trigger and diode nib of the *PummelFist*. The smart and light, but ugly contraption, was a very powerful weapon in the hands of the officers of the Security Corps.

The *PummelFist* collapsed together as Hallow held his hand under the vice. Clicking off another control it dropped into the palm of his hand. Hallow held it gingerly as he motioned to DuSalle to take it.

The Detective took the weapon, gripping the bulb tightly. The weapon emitted a soft beep as it accepted his palm print and heat signature.

"That's yours now, Detective," said Hallow. "No one else but you can use it."

They left the SWT room after the final calibrations were made to the advanced *PummelFist* to DuSalle's specs.

"I'm afraid that I have other duties, Detective," said Cartier, as they rode the ascend shaft once more. "So I shall have to leave you on your floor. But the Chief has an assignment already for you."

DuSalle frowned. "Am I not to meet my partner first, Sir?"

"I'm sure you will in the short term, Detective." They shook hands as the door hissed open to DuSalle's floor. "I have a feeling we'll meet again. 'Til then, Detective." Then Cartier was gone leaving DuSalle with the odd feeling that they might indeed meet again.

As the doors closed behind him, DuSalle came upon a different sort of bustling, officers carrying precariously piled plastic files and data-discs in their arms.

He followed several directions on the walls until he came upon a faux-oak double door. The dull morning glow hazed through the inlayed misted glass on which was printed in bold black:

'TALVIN A. VICE,
QUADRANT CHIEF,
E. 242'

DuSalle knocked assertively on the faux-wood. There was a click and the doors slid smoothly aside to reveal the shadowy office beyond.

"Come in," said Chief Vice. The dim red light of the morning filtered through the blinds, creating a silhouette of the Quad Chief. The glow of his console screen was the only other light in the room, highlighting his craggy features and the streaks of grey at his temples. "Cartier's been showing you round, Detective?"

"Yes, Sir. I have my new equipment," answered DuSalle, to which Vice acknowledged with only a slight nod. DuSalle took a breath before he continued. "Sir, I would like to ask – why was I transferred here?"

"First of all, Detective," said Chief Vice, speaking as though he had not heard DuSalle, though studying him with hooded but intense eyes. "I am not going to give the 'welcome to the team' speech, because until I see positive results in the work you do in these Quads, whatever has been said about you elsewhere, there is no point in being pre-emptive about it. Your previous Quad Chief considered, however, that you would need a change of pace. Being a Detective is much different to being a Constable. This is not the simple Street Section now. You are no longer part of a riot strike team, stumbling about through the fields, chasing simple plant thieves. Your commission here in the Eastern Quads will be a tough one, especially with me in charge. If you complete one year of being a detective, DuSalle, then maybe and only maybe will you be able to atomise the cheese paste with me." DuSalle opened his mouth to speak again, but the Chief vice carried on. "In answer to your other question, you're being partnered with Inspector Jase Chapel."

"I see," said DuSalle carefully. "And when do I meet the Inspector, Sir?"

"Currently," said Chief Vice, a flicker of something crossed his face, almost similar to the look that had crossed Cartier's face, he leant back in his swivel chair. "He's undercover, solving some puzzler of a case, with a Trainee as I understand from my sources. You should find him in some dive pilot's bar or something of that description on the outskirts of the Docks. I've had Control uploaded the information into your assigned patrol car's computer. You'll need to sign for it. Dismissed, Detective."

"Thank you, Sir." He turned to leave the office.

"Detective," called Vice, not taking his eyes from his console. "One thing you should know – about the Inspector I mean."

"Yes, Sir?"

"Expect anything."

"Yes, Sir." He nodded as the door closed.

DuSalle rode a descend shaft to the patrol carpool, collecting and signing for the key card from the attendant before driving out the sleek purple patrol vehicle. He asked the car's computer to map out the locations of the various pilot's bars around the docks that were compiled in the list. The day's ground traffic swallowed him up.

II

"Are you sure you know how it works?"

Constable Chloe Warren snapped awake. Relief flooded her to be out of that nightmare and back safe and comfortable in her Quad Base's dorm, lying in her own bed. In few hours she would be on patrol and then after, when she was off duty go to meet him again at the –

With a jolt she realised she wasn't in her dorm.

As the shaven-haired Constable traced back her last memories she could hear voices, inaudible just on the edge of her listening range.

She had been chasing a man she had caught trying to place a device in Kelter Street, just off the *Flayed Dragon*. She had followed him into an alleyway and he had caught her off guard. Now she was his prisoner.

But not for long.

She reached out for her weapon to find her hands and arms couldn't move. The young Constable also discovered that she had been stripped of her armour and uniform. She was virtually naked, with no armour to protect her and no weapons to defend herself.

Chloe was laid out on a leather-topped table. The top of her head was held in place by an invisible force and she had difficulty in closing her eyes. She was trapped. She didn't bother to talk, just strained to hear, as she could distantly hear voices coming towards her through the shell of her dark and blurry enclosure.

"This is a work of genius," said a voice, cultured and measured, familiar. "Six months of getting this out under the Security Corp's nose, piece by bloody piece. Do you think I would be stupid enough to not find out how it works?"

"Your services were well acquired," said a second voice, gruff but respectful, "but don't think it gains you any latitude with me."

"Yes, you may have done your bit, but don't think we trust you yet," said a third voice, sounding smugly condescending. "Now it's our show."

"As long as it's not off-world filth," said the second voice, "then I'm perfectly happy to… look she's awake."

"Good," said the first voice. The young constable thought for a moment. She recognised that voice, she was sure she did. "Now let's try it out."

"Adjusting now," said the second voice.

She wasn't sure what was going on, but it involved the isolationists, which she sure that was not a good thing. What was this machine they going to use on her? She didn't like the sound of it and tied to move, but it was useless.

Was it mind-control? she wondered.

There weren't many ways of stopping mind control. The young Constable suspected that the Judicial Internal Section held these secrets back. After all they didn't want probable rogue officers defeating their machines.

"My name is Constable Chloe Warren, of South Quad Base 89," she bellowed. It was just about possible to shout. The pressure on top of her, increased slightly.

"I wouldn't do that, Chloe," said the third voice. "This is gravity vice that is holding you down, it can be increased to –"

"My name is Constable Chloe Warren, of South Quad Base 89," she repeated, loudly. "My name is Constable Chloe Warren, of South Quad Base 89."

"Very well," said the third voice, over hers. "Do it!"

Suddenly an image appeared before her eyes. It was a small single bright dot. Warren simply gazed at it, repeating her litany over and over, as loud as she could. Then the dot grew larger and larger until it filled her entire world. Her litany got quieter and quieter as the dot increased in size.

Then it was in her head, consuming her.

The light went out.

Warren took a deep breath and without warning, there was a suddenly flurry of pictures.

She could hardly try to blink before there was a second flurry of pictures.

The pictures now occupied Warren's mind. They brought up certain images within her. She tried to continue her litany.

...My name is Constable Chloe Warren, of South Quad Base 89, my name is Constable Chloe Warren, of South Quad Base 89, my name is Constable Chloe Warren, of South Quad Base 89, my name is Constable Chloe Warren.

She remembered things she hadn't thought of in years. When she was eight she had got lost in the dark streets of the Southern Quads, her father had died before she was even one, and her mother, seemingly tottering into insanity, dressed her in a pink skirt and pigtails. She had travelled three miles, missing the street gangs, but she was almost attacked by a bunch of hiding criminals, who were discovered by the Security Corps and she was taken back home. The attackers had been off-worlders...

...My name is Constable Chloe Warren, of South Quad, my name is Constable Chloe Warren, of South Quad, my name is Constable Chloe Warren, of South Quad, my name is Constable Chloe Warren...

At the age of ten, she was co-opted into the Security Corps, a fate that is bestowed upon many of the orphaned children of the city, but first they have to pass through ten years of rigorous instruction at the Security Training School.

The dark, shadowy streets amongst the metropolis of Chandler City were terrifying to enter even with company, so training was made ten times tougher. Boys and girls of nine or ten were ordered by old lightly garbed Senseis to undress and stand naked in a line. Anybody messing around was hit with a stun truncheon across the backside or taken out of the line at once.

Put on a conveyor like a slab of meat, the new recruits were given extreme medical checks, their hair was completely shaved off and they were measured for their uniforms. Further along several more would-be recruits were taken out because of bad behaviour, or their medical charts showed them not fit to step into duty. Then they were fitted into dorms, some mixed or single sex and then told to dress into their rough uniforms and meet on the grounds.

The training itself was harsh. Out of the three hundred children that had started on the conveyor, seventy were taken out for behaviour and another twelve for bad health problems. Passing through the training had taken out fifty-three and six died on the courses themselves.

The hundred and fifty-nine left went on to further training for the next ten years. Chloe Warren earned her first scar to the back of her upper left thigh from the first day of stun-truncheon combat training. There were hardly any holidays and if there were they were short and the recruit was kept busy.

Over the years, she gained many other scars, but the one that would stick in her mind was her first. This was a scar she had earned in a brutal and bruising clash outside of class, a girl who attacked her for no reason, who had survived the harshness of the School, but wanted no part of it.

An off-worlder...

…My name is Chloe Warren, of South Quad, my name is Chloe Warren, of South Quad, my name is Chloe Warren, of South Quad, my name is Chloe Warren…

Now she had been at the school for six years.

She earned a scar to her left hand from a laser bolt, grazing her in a practice, going with the scar on her thigh, a third on her foot from walking bare-footed across broken glass and hot burning logs.

Her training had brought to her routine, but this was constantly interrupted by violent outbursts of practice or punishments, that took place if a recruit was messing up. 'If one of your unit messes up, you all mess up and you all take the consequences…" their Drill–Sensei was fond of saying.

But after this time, with what she had been told, taught and brought here to learn, this would now be tested in a simulated situation. With intricacy designed holographic streets and characters created in the training arena, even though it was virtual simulation, injuries could be very real to the person wearing the helmet and suit.

Of the hundred and fifty-nine that had made it through the first day of tests and training, eight were killed by the off-world girl. There were now one hundred and fifty, and this test was the greatest cull of all. Once, of originally two hundred and twelve that had made it that far, only sixty-two remained afterwards. Most of the fortunate recruits had lost two limbs or a hand or foot. The unfortunate were buried with full Security Corps recruit rights.

This was a live round test – the last of three, but the toughest.

It was a test of many things, to do with character, skill and toughness. To this test there were three levels, but they were intermixed with the situations that she would be confronted with.

The arena was the best test of all. They were dressed into the 'nerve' suit, which acted like the armoured suit of the Security Corps officer, the protective level of which was controlled by the assessor.

She was brought straight into the action with fiery bolts of energy already flying toward her face. She managed to dodge them and take cover beside a Corps vehicle. She took out two of the seven firing on her, telling the animated Corps officers to cover her as she went into the building to sort out the problem. Her armour had been up at ninety percent. By the end of the session it was down to fifty-seven, her weapon had only three charges and one of the three animated officers had been killed of the twelve shooters, eight had been killed and the others were arrested.

No sooner had this finished then she was sweating, breathing hard and almost worn out, and was brought into a second situation. Her armour went down to twenty-five. If she had lost more than fifty points on her armour in the last round, it would have been ten.

Three criminals and two hostages. The criminals were armed with heavy weaponry, stolen for a cache of Corps weapons. Yells of the hostages and growls of the criminals filled her ears, her gun hand was raised in the direction of the leader, she was shouting at her to drop it, she was flanked by only one back-up, who had already dropped his weapon.

She lowered her weapon slowly, sweat dripped off her nose, then she raised it and fired at the centre criminal. Her back-up killed the one of the right and she fired at the one on the left but missed, injuring the hostage instead who yelled in pain, but she had no time to stop. She dodged a laser bolt, fired at the criminal again, who dodged, the back-up fired, but smashed a window. The criminal stood up, aiming his weapon, but too late. She fired, decapitating the criminal, the body slumping to the floor as the head flew backwards out the window.

Her body aching, sweat making the suit slick against her skin, she was thrown into the third and last situation.

She had no armour this time and she was on her own. She looked around, noting also that she had enough charge in the weapon for four shots.

She was in a dark alleyway. She stopped and listened.

Spinning around, she fired and a body slumped to her feet. She now had three bolts left to use.

A bolt split the air and she dove for cover behind a pile of old garbage, the smell made the simulation take on a new form. She fired one bolt into the darkness, then sitting back she listened.

Then she heard it, spun around and fired her two remaining charges and the body collapsed into view. The world suddenly swirled into complete black.

"Very good," said a voice in her ear, as she stared blankly around the open arena. "A very good score, Trainee Warren. You show great promise." Her heart soared. "Topped only by Trainee Farra, who scored ninety-eight points." The bottom dropped out of her stomach.

Farra, an off-worlder …

…My name is Chloe Warren, my name is Chloe Warren, my name is Chloe Warren, my name is Chloe Warren…

Nine years of training had now passed and she would be tested in the real thing.

Her assessor was Chief Inspector Jacob Hart, only the second hard examiner in the Security Corps. The top one was Inspector Blackthorn, a tough man who had only passed twelve of the twenty-one recruits he had assessed. Jacob Hart, a large burly man of fifty-two, had only passed six of his fourteen assessments.

She was certainly nervous, just like the other fifty-two that had made it to the final year of the Security Corps Training School, six of which had made it onto the honour roll of the class of '37.

The recruits were called out and taken in the patrol cars by their Instructor–Senseis. Chloe ended up with Jacob Hart. It was not as bad as she had first feared. Of course that fear never showed on her face – it had not been shown openly for nine years now. The test would go on as long as the instructor deemed fit. Hart had once taken out a recruit for almost seven months before he gave him a top mark.

To begin with it was a routine day and she was called out to seven public disturbances, a robbery and a few jaywalkers.

Having been trained in both the 3D simulators and the live round practice arenas, she had become adapted to the lively fast pace of a weapon battle or simply subduing a suspect so they would not be able to stick a knife between the padding of your armour.

In each situation, where they were present, Hart asked her probing questions about procedure, rules from the book and the ideal protocol to defuse various hostile situations. Even when they were shot at, slits of light passing over their heads, ozone clotting the air with shouts and screams all around, he asked her a question and she answered it as best she could.

It was only three days later, when they were caught in a cross fire between two enraged café owners, that she was given the rank of Constable on the spot. As the body of one of the owners was catered off, Chloe arrested the battered survivor.

He was an off-worlder…

…My name is Chloe Warren, my name is Chloe Warren, my name is Chloe Warren, my name is Chloe Warren…

Chloe was on patrol alone for the first time in six months.

Her current partner was in laser traction for a week, due to a major hostage fiasco below Delwin's Flyway. She had taken the patrol car out, hoping for a call to action.

Instead she had been coasting close to *La Flayed Dragon* when she spotted a fight in the alleyway. Turning on her sirens she pulled her *Enforcer* patrol car onto the pavement, then she grabbed her *PummelFist* from the holster next to the driving column and leapt out of the car.

"This is the Security Corps!" she called. "Freeze and desist!"

The two men stopped fighting. Chloe's eyes widened behind her goggles as the taller, rather dapperly dressed and handsome human stood, the leather-clad and ugly looking human sprawled under him.

"Officer, I'm glad you arrived," the handsome man said. "My name is Clove. I was just exiting this rather interesting establishment when this man jumped me."

"I – I see," stuttered Chloe. "You on your feet!" she ordered the mohawk-haired man. "Against the patrol car."

Clove moved forward. Had Chloe had her wits about her, she would have been affronted by the invasion of her personal space.

"Again, thank you. Constable is it?"

"Yes," she breathed. "It's Constable Chloe Warren." The closeness of Clove caused a jump in Chloe's heartbeat. "You were dining at *La Flayed Dragon*?"

Clove smiled warmly. "Yes, I was. I was made aware they serve a delicious Ai'tolian dish. I was just returning to my office when our mutual friend here attacked me."

Chloe looked Clove over, telling herself she was checking him for any injuries, but knowing that she was just checking him out. Then she produced cuffs from utility belt. Clove quirked an eyebrow, while Chloe blushingly cuffed the criminal and threw him in the back seat of the car.

"Do you lunch at The Dragon often?" asked Chloe.

"It seems to be a popular place," said Clove, still smiling. "I just might return."

"Good," said Chloe, returning the smile.

Clove, she later found, as she shared his bed, was an off-worlder…

…My name is unimportant but I serve the People's Island…

III

La Flayed Dragon was well into its fourth 'Happy Hour' when DuSalle took his introductory step into the gaudy Astral Pilot's discotheque.

From under the peak of his newly-fitted cap, DuSalle cast his blue eyes over the dim interior, where the retro-metallic look of the bar was at odds with the wooden flooring of the dance area.

This was the third location that Quad Control had given him to find his irritatingly elusive partner.

The elevated DJ podium was pumping out bellowing tones of the latest tracks, as the various species of the colonised galaxy danced to the thumping beat.

A few metres away, on the other side of the railed off and brightly lit disco floor, the more travelled and less social Stels, as many Chandler residence called people from off-world, huddled in the corner booths, swapping drunken space tales.

The Detective rolled his shoulders as he moved toward his target, the description of Chapel fixed in his mind as he scanned the various patrons of *La Flayed Dragon*.

There were no overtly real criminal types clutching at the border–lying docking bays and ports of Chandler City. Most were independent opportunists who operated more in the intersection of trade and industrial progress, rather than out and out criminality. Most of them were slapped with a few fines and taxes, or at the more extreme end, they were exiled from Chandler City space entirely.

That was as far as Chandler City law went. While they could boast confidently about the seemingly inefficient restrictions, they were never in a hurry to return.

DuSalle had strongly agreed with this tactic. While the isolationist groups griped about kid gloves, the unionists were applauding it. Their governments would deal with them while the Security Corps dealt with domestic problems.

Since the arrival of the massively prosperous Stellar Sovereignty and the relatively meagre inspection fleets of Pastoral Regions, crime had been on the increase. As with many things involved in import or export, bringing in a number of rather unsavoury privateers and illicit dealings, the Security Corps was more confident and adept at handling these goings on than it had been at the start. They were after all loose knit gangs, clinging together out of self-interest, which extended into them selling each other out rather than risk lengthy sentences in the cells, as DuSalle himself had bared witness to such weakness of character in their 'masterminds'.

Amongst the Five Species, the Quazians, the first race that humans had encountered, tall and pale-skinned with large bulbous heads and slanted black liquid eyes, of marvellous intellect and patience, were rarely seen in these parts of the city. Mostly the Ai'tol, a sea dwelling race, always encased in suits and helmets, or Rkanan's, an insect like species, and the occasional human were present around the trading centres, selling various knock-off wares or illegal transcriptions, something DuSalle had dealt with easily before his last near disastrous case in the Western Quads landed him here as Detective.

As DuSalle passed several tables, a spirited conversation ceased between a bearded Rkanan, whose limbs ceased failing, and an overly scarred young human, his smug features suddenly set in a grim but otherwise unreadable expression.

Another table was hushed as he past, glasses clinking on tabletops as two huddled Ai'tolians, their streamlined, jowly features encased in fish bowl helmets filled with the florescent purple liquid of their homeworld to assist in their breathing, stopped speaking through their head mic's. Their large globular eyes rotated in high anxiety. The Detective simply ignored them all, his mind set on his one task.

When he spotted a hunched shadow at the back of the bar, a certain part of relief and final trepidation overcame him.

"You there, got ID?" asked DuSalle.

The hunched figure belched and pulled itself from its slumped position for DuSalle to see a wrinkly old man with a scarred bulbous nose and dull blue eyes, peering out from a matted mop of grey hair and beard, collapsed half in his seat over a glass tumbler of oily black sickly smelling liquid.

"Wha' yer want?" muttered the scraggy figure, between chapped lips and stained teeth. DuSalle, despite the faint rotting odour, leaned in closer, trying to shake off the hint of embarrassment at what he was about to say to a probable drunken stranger.

"The stars are brighter from the southern point," said DuSalle in lowered tones, using the formatted code that Quad Chief Vice had given him, in order to attract Security Corp operatives notice, holding in his astonishment at the dishevelled appearance of the man who was to be partnered to him.

He had heard stories about the rather infamous Inspector from the Eastern Quads, but not that he was a drunk.

The set of the man's ancient features seemed to harden for a moment as he cast his watery gaze over DuSalle's tall frame and then over the Detective's broad shoulder.

He belched again, raising his arm, crooked a stubby finger from his grubby fingerless leather gloves at the Detective.

DuSalle moved closer to the possible-Inspector. The smell was almost tangible to the Detective now.

"Excuse me, Sir?" The hunched man was unresponsive, staring into the bottom of his half empty glass.

DuSalle's anger and frustration about the last few days which had laid back in his unconsciousness waiting to be released during a training exercise, could not be denied now.

The Detective felt his eyebrows draw down together.

"WAKE UP, YOU DRUNK OLD SOD!"

"But they are better viewed from the east, are they not, Constable?" came the counter-code finally, though this time it was in a clear and more certain voice. DuSalle stared at the Inspector, his anger draining away instantly, as though he were a completely different person.

"I am Detective DuSalle, Sir –" With whiplash speed the Inspector grabbed DuSalle's collar, hauling him closer.

"No time for introductions, Constable," he whispered harshly, the stink invading DuSalle. "Now that's out of the way with, would you mind stepping into the background, as a rather important supplier is about to make his appearance. If he is not arrested in an orderly fashion, seven months of work will be destroyed."

"Sir." DuSalle complied instantly, his training taking over any other concerns of the moment. As the Inspector let go, DuSalle moved himself behind Chapel's table, deeper in the shadows.

The main doors opened, and in strode a rather squat, barrel-chested Drylian, dressed in blue shipping technician's grease stained garb, his green mottled skin glistening from the heat, which for the majority of other species in the bar was merely comfortable.

He made his way through the bustling people and to the bar, where he ordered a drink.

DuSalle watched this unhurried performance tensely, though Inspector Chapel seemed unconcerned. In fact he was throwing back the last dregs of his Quazian black ale with the gusto of a stern alcoholic, which made DuSalle even more uncomfortable.

Though he was armed with a stun truncheon and his newly formatted *PummelFist* sidearm, the unease of the situation would not disappear.

Then when DuSalle's impatience was readying him to leap out of the shadows and arrest the Drylian for simply wasting the Security Corps time, the Inspector's prey finally ambled up to the table.

Chapel burped loudly as the Drylian approached. Large bloodshot silver eyes gazed sharply at Chapel. DuSalle balled his fists. This Drylian was too rigid in his movements, which indicated to DuSalle that he had taken something before the meeting.

The Drylian civilisation, who were the third to be in contact with the human race two thousand years ago, still retained their easy flowing movements of the aquatic ancestry, except this Drylian, who seemed to be riding some sort of high.

DuSalle thought through the list of narcotics and stimulants, which could cause this effect in Drylians, but none seemed to come to mind.

Though the Detective was sure he was unnoticeable to the creature's poor night vision, he sunk further back into the shadows.

"Ah ha... Kybrant, my lad!" exclaimed Chapel, chuckling drunkenly. "Glad you could... join... meet... me."

"That's Kybrint, Cable. Keep yer voice down, will ya? Ya drunken old fool." Kybrint sat down heavily, the wire frame chair creaking softly. "How can you drink such filth?" he asked, pulling a disgusted face at Chapel's glass.

"I have... I have the constitution of a Mouse–Hound, Kybrint, my lad. I am very cap... capa... Able to meet with you." Chapel beamed drunkenly.

"Have you got the 'urple?" asked Kybrint moving closer, turning serious. DuSalle tried to stop himself again from leaping up, trying in vain to do what his Inspector had ordered him to do.

"I've got the money, yes, my lad, 'non probis' as the Shippers say, eh?" Chapel chuckled.

"That's Ai'tol flange, Cable, I don't abide of that! Not after the heavy fines they shift on us folk earnin' our livin'," said Kybrint gruffly, with only a small amount of disgust, moved closer to the Inspector so to not be closely overheard, which greatly annoyed DuSalle.

Though DuSalle knew little of the Shipping Confederation, being educated in the barest economic stats of the Stels or Pastorals, he had gleaned certain info on the small uncoordinated smuggling gangs which operated around the farm lands.

A disorganised rabble as they always were, whatever their old sayings it was nothing but hot air to the Detective.

They continued to speak in hurried whispers for several minutes. DuSalle was again fighting to sit still, not able to listen in to a conversation that was barely a metre away.

Then the rather underdressed waitress with blue tinted skin and shocking neon green hair moved up to their table. The plotting pair split from their secretive conversation as she lay down the drinks that Kybrint had ordered from the bar.

"Thanks doll," said Chapel, grinning with yellow-grey teeth, then gave the girl a tap on the behind.

Kybrint gave him another disgusted look as the waitress sashayed way.

"So that's the way it is... though I was able to get past a small sample," continued Kybrint, taking a large gulp from the florescent yellow liquid in the tumbler. "Got it right through, under the very noses of those damned uptight eunuchs of the Security Corps." He laughed.

As DuSalle watched, his blue eyes narrowing, the smuggler pulled a small pouch from his pocket as Chapel lifted a case from under his chair on to the table.

"Heh, really? Yeah, s'pose those chumps are really easy, ain't they?" Chapel grinned broadly.

Kybrint grimaced again. Though DuSalle knew the Inspector was playing a part, he thought he detected a hint of sincerity in Chapel's rough voice.

"Yeah," said Kybrint, his eyes drawn to the case, as he took another sip from his drink. The Inspector saluted with his glass and drank the dregs. "Yer look like yer could use the money. This stuff'll get you millions 'ere."

"That's very good, Mr. Kybrint, very good," said Chapel, straightening up, as his voice became more and more sober, less ragged and more refined. "You are now under arrest for drug smuggling. Do you understand?"

Kybrint stared at Chapel for a split second in disbelief, then with lethal speed reached into his jacket, only to have a *PummelFist* at his neck, held by the neon green haired waitress. "How did you–"

"Easy, Mr. Kybrint," said Chapel, no longer smiling drunkenly. "Constable Staves here is training with the Narcotics Unit, and has successfully managed to bag her first arrest. As such, she has an itchy trigger thumb, as you may understand, Mr. Kybrint. Good work, Constable, good work! Would you not say so, DuSalle? Chief Vice will receive my report of your progress by the morning."

Constable Staves nodded briskly and proceeded to manhandle the stunned Drylian out of his chair and into a pair of handcuffs which she seemed to have produced from thin air, DuSalle could not imagine where she had been able to conceal it on her less than concealing attire.

Chapel turned unconcernedly to DuSalle, as he quickly emerged from the shadows. "Now Detective, exactly what…"

Suddenly, Kybrint leapt out of Stave's grip, the table crashing aside as he brandished a small pocket laser at Chapel.

The Inspector moved with such lightning speed that DuSalle was only able to gape as the Drylian dove towards them.

Chapel moved out of the plunging blade's way, caught Kybrint by the wrist and twisted hard, thrusting a back-handed elbow into the Drylian's face.

"Well, that certainly makes it harder," huffed Chapel, turning to Staves as Kybrint crumpled to the floor. The Inspector kicked the cutter away from the Drylian's reach, picking it up. "I doubt this will make a difference though, Constable. After all he didn't even scratch me. I think he'll be quiet from now on. Just have to call in for a wagon." A flicker of mirth passed over Chapel's grotesque features as he handed over the cutter to Staves. The Inspector turned back to DuSalle. "I think we'll finish this outside, Detective. As they say in your Western Quads, 'flame is not always where the fire begins', yes?"

"Er… yes, Sir. Yes that's right, Sir," said DuSalle weakly, he followed Inspector Chapel outside *La Flayed Dragon*.

VI

The Security Corps' patrol vehicle, as DuSalle had read early on in Basic Engineering Manual (10yr), was fully equipped with the latest technologically advanced hardware and software of Pelimar's brightest specialists. The majority of it was based on the original specifications of the Unity Enforcement Traverser.

On the outside, this was at least true.

After the Reconsolidation, along with many long debates within and without the Chamber of Patrons, the Security Corps and the Municipal Militia were given the authorisation to confiscate arms and equipment from impounded craft for the ultimate defence of Chandler City.

After several hundred years without contact to the rest of the expanding colonies and the empires that arose, the city's independence had created a unity within the government and the established policing force, which would strive to overcome and outclass the expanded though crude criminal element that was now flowing into its ports.

In its infancy it had not been easy, but by combatting each problem as it arose, the Security Corps was now a solid routine of adjustment and augmentation.

"Isn't this the old *Trigger* series, Sir?" DuSalle looked over the grey interior of the vehicle, noting the old style oak finish to the dashboard, which was scuffed and worn, the radio and handset leaking multi-coloured wiring like spilt worms over the gear stick. "I thought they were disbanded after the *Enforcer* series?"

"Yes, they were, Detective," said Chapel, not turning from watching the steady flow of sky traffic in front of them. "But I like the older Trigger series. This is the J type I believe, they stopped commissioning after the L type, though it should have stopped at K, it was more robust."

"I thought the new series was available here in the metropolis, Sir," said DuSalle, making more of a question out of it than a statement.

"Your point, Detective?"

"I was –"

"What were you saying, Detective?" asked Chapel, cutting in with a slightly amused look, though still with his eye on the traffic. "I am well aware of the new series, but I have made a few upgrades to this system. I found it easier to do any repair work that was needed myself. I've had this vehicle a long time. It hasn't done me wrong yet, though if it does, I may upgrade properly."

"Sir, I just meant that –"

"'To fight crime, one does not need to upgrade his technology but to upgrade his subtlety', Sergeant Major Samstone, Directive four point five–one of the Security Corps Training Rule Manual, Year Three, old issue," Quoted Chapel. "Though I think that was edited down a bit in the new edition. I haven't had a read of it as yet."

The old-style patrol car flew in silence across the skyline through tubular tunnels which connected the massive domes together and out the other side to the destination Chapel had desired to visit.

The Inspector brought the vehicle over a double line of traffic and into a break between two Stakk-Flats as the sky lights changed to red.

"So, Chief Vice has seen fit to lumber me with a new Street Detective?" asked Chapel, as he drummed his fingers on the controls.

"That's correct, Sir," said DuSalle formally. "I've been assigned to you as of this morning, Sir."

"Well, since you are under my orders, that's a good thing," said The Inspector. "Unless you are like the thugs about, that is."

"Sir," responded DuSalle, with as much respect as he could muster.

"Yes, you really are green aren't you?" said Chapel, scowling. This made his gnarled features look even more awful than they were already. "In fact, I need to make a short stop before we get back."

"Where to, Sir? The Chief did say –"

"The Chief is a busy man, Detective," said Chapel, cutting him off, "as are all Quad Chiefs what with the celebrations coming up, the P.I.M. seeming to re–new their bombing campaign and the G.A.I.A. street parties. But this brief stopover to the Envoy Building will take but a minute."

"The Envoy Building, Sir?" said DuSalle, confused.

"Let me show you." Chapel sighed, tapping the on–board console to the GPS system.

Then he touched another contact, which seemed not to be of the same style of the SC Tech design of the patrol car, and the bolted-on holo'plate in the front window glowed to life. A long stream of purple flashed up, superimposed on the wind shield, seeming to stretch out in front of them as if the patrol car was on a rail to their destination.

DuSalle was awestruck for a moment, having not seen this before in the more rural Western Quads. The Detective did not have to look over at the Inspector to tell that Chapel was waiting for him to act like a frightened Trainee.

Chapel landed the patrol car outside a tall, grey and rather uninspiring government building.

"I suppose I better not go in looking like this," Chapel murmured, almost to himself.

Before DuSalle could even think as to what to say to this, Chapel threw off his hair, that was in reality a ruffled and matted wig and peeled off the wrinkled features and gnarled prosthetic gloves to reveal a rather prominent and crooked nose, which had been broken at some point in the past, a strong almost lantern-like jaw which had been covered in mass of wrinkles, scars and warts. Light brown, almost white hair which was swept back from the face now replaced the tangled mane. He peeled the wrinkled skin from his long thin fingers.

"You looked surprised, Detective," said Chapel, balling up the disguise and shoving it into the glove box, then massaging his face. "I have a thing for disguises. It has always been that way when on assignment, this however is my real face, not some hobo drunk, I hope you didn't think that was the real me?" DuSalle heard the challenge in the older man's voice.

"Of course not, Sir. I knew that you were undercover," he lied.

The phantom smile tugged the corners of Chapel's thin-lipped mouth, though on his face it was less obvious, as his features were sans wrinkles now. "Of course. Let's go and get this over with. I shall be as fast as I can, Detective," he said, smiling more obviously this time. "Don't just sit there gawping, Detective. Make the call, then."

DuSalle shakily picked up the hand receiver and contacted the Envoy Building's main reception.

While DuSalle spoke automatically into the handset, he thought how he had heard all of the stories of the infamous Inspector Chapel.

Most of it was wild rumour, having been called many things in the mess halls or locker-rooms. However there was one that had been left out and DuSalle wanted dearly for it to be added to the list: extremely troublesome.

They were given a port on the eastern side. Upon landing on the sun drenched grid, Chapel and DuSalle exited their patrol car.

With Chapel taking the lead, they strolled across the landing grid. His large grey padded but worn trench coat, which he had pulled over the technicians overalls, swished and swirled about his tall gaunt frame.

"Now, Detective," said Chapel, as they entered the building, "I'm going to answer a few of the questions I know are burning inside of you." DuSalle followed slightly behind as Chapel seemed to know the lay out of the building. "But Conduct of an Officer, such as it is worth these days, prevents you from asking." Chapel smirked as DuSalle attempted to school his expression far and away from a frown of contempt he wished to display. "A diplomat of some standing, fairly new around here, made it a hobby to visit La Flayed Dragon on various occasions, maybe to take in the scenery or under-the-table-dealings or just simply to procure illegal drugs." Chapel went on. The buckles on his sleeves jingled slightly as he moved past the rather sparse looking main foyer, spotted with small overly bright and leafy potted plants in the corners, possibly from the Dome Walls or expensively imported. DuSalle was no botanical expert to be sure of them, growing up grey pseudo-marble pillars, to the info-Netbase by the lobby ascend shaft at the far end of the small waiting room.

"That is not of importance at this time." He set about typing in a name. "What was important was that he was one of several witnesses to a kidnapping of a Security Corps officer. A Constable sure, but still an officer is an officer and we have need of everyone. Aha, there he is, so follow me, Detective."

DuSalle followed Chapel's purposeful strides into the ascend shaft.

"Floor Please," said the dead-tone voice of the Beneficial government central Ascend/Descend comp-net.

"Override Gamma–Venus five, Chapel, Inspector Jase, clearance pattern Delta. Repeat, override Gamma-Venus five, pattern Delta."

"Accepted Inspector, which level do you require?" asked the ascend shaft in a more polite tone than before.

"Floor 218, Section 5, Beta," stated Chapel quickly, leading DuSalle to think this was not the first time the Inspector had said it.

The Detective did not understand why Chapel would wait until this moment to use it, unless the Inspector wanted to delay his assignment.

The continuation of any current case was seldom when a new member was entered into the team, especially as Chapel seemed to be holding all the leads to it.

"Ascending." The shaft jolted to life and ticked off the floors.

"Right, Detective, here's what I want you to do when we are up there to interview my witness," said Chapel turning to DuSalle, his face seemed to be suddenly alive. The pallor of his skin seemed to have gained a brighter sheen and his dull eyes were lit with an inner fire as he spoke. "I want you to take in every detail around you, understand? The man's secretary, how she dresses, the way her desk is arranged, the man's office, the desk arrangement, the walls, his clothing, everything. Yes? Understand that, Detective?"

"Er... err... yes. Yes, Sir. Of course, Sir," answered DuSalle, to Chapel's battering ram of orders. "Should I have my notebook, Sir?"

A shadow seemed to pass over Chapel's face.

"No, Detective," he sighed. "No, I have a 'corder. Just do as I ordered, and I'm sure you will, to the best of your sufficient abilities, complete your job." Chapel turned his back on the Detective as they rode the ascend shaft in a cool silence.

As they exited the shaft, DuSalle was running on an adrenalin thrum. He took in all the detail of the corridor, as he followed Chapel, who seemed to know very well where he was going, at a rapid pace.

Chapel suddenly turned, DuSalle blundering behind him, as he burst into the outer officer of the secretary who was dressed in a subdued grey pinstripe one suit with puffed up sleeves, her black hair in ringlets around her large brown eyes, which scowled from over her rather pristine desk as they entered.

"Yes, can I – you can't go in there, Sir! – Who are you? – Stop!"

Chapel did not stop, as he pushed passed the irate secretary. "My name is unimportant at this point, Miss Bonnel. My business with your boss, however, is." DuSalle moved to intercept her as Chapel threw open the door to the inner office.

"Mr. –" he stopped.

DuSalle turned from the furious secretary. Chapel had stopped on the verge of the office interior.

He rushed over, his head seeming to spin, as he took in the cabinets along the walls of the small office, the large wall of window letting in the afternoon sun, the wooden desk, with transparent papers strewn over it and the console screen smashed on the floor.

The man that Inspector Chapel came to see lay inertly sprawled forward over his desk, dead.

DuSalle's vision went dark.

V

Prenbrett Sullivan realised he was running late when Mrs Brackyn holo'ed him.

She rang on the dot of three quarter, Eastern Quad time, where he was usually playing four tier chess with his upper-Stakk mates and would not be in to receive her calls.

He hated to just ignore the holo', but knew that if he pressed the 'Answer' tab, he was in for a three hour lecture on 'my husband's infected something or other' or if it was the weekend, 'My something or other cousin from South Quad brought up a something or other present which was most kind, though not really welcome, blah, blah, etc., etc.'.

When Sullivan had immigrated from the other side of the galaxy, Chandler City seemed like a new and different change of pace than Terra Sovereign, where he was merely a seventh level filing clerk for Xavier Dynasty's massive and overwielding Administration Department.

Sullivan looked back from the open doorway, the fluorescent blue light buzzing and flickering, to the corridor where his holo'receiver sat on the rickety plastic table, one of the first things he had bought when he had arrived in the city, the 'call arriving' diode beeping on and off.

He turned on his booted heel. His black shoulder length hair ruffled slightly, as his door slid shut and locked behind him.

Shoving his fisted hands deep into his yellow padded jacket, while sticking his metallic playing board under his arm, he shuddered slightly.

The Stakk-Flat Maintenance Union was on strike again, about pay or rates, or probably just laziness, depending on what day of the month it was.

Sullivan had lost track as it happened so often. Internal heating and supplies were not affected as such, but as soon as you stepped into the corridors, the chill struck you to the bone.

Sullivan took a descend shaft down toward Lower-Stakk Common Level, having to change over three floors down as the north descend shaft was in need of repair.

The doors to the second descend swept open to admit him, graffiti scrawled on the back wall. A young woman, with razor cut auburn hair, dressed in a grey suit and large boots, a vacant expression on her finely shaped features, entered behind him.

Then her sharp brown eyes met his green. Sullivan knew that look. As an 'off–worlder', one of the kinder phrases he had heard, he was looked upon with slight suspicion and contempt. It seemed to be more relaxed in the West and North Quads, but East Quads were uneven, living in dome-scraping warrens of striking officials and grubby streets, while many of the 'Stels' in their feudal daze lived in near opulence. Sullivan was not surprised by the hostility.

He flexed his fingers in his pockets, an old nervous habit he'd picked up from weeks of Acclimatisation in the Quarantine House, before being formally inserted as a resident here, as the lighter atmosphere made his rather portly frame near buoyant than on Earth.

Sullivan turned his back on the scowling woman. As the doors enclosed them, pressing the button for his floor, something tickled around his mind, as he looked at the graffiti tag of the Pitt, a gang of local kids that the Security Corps could never get a lock onto, vicious and unruly teens roaming the streets and the Stakks for food, money, or for the simple lust to kill. It was probably about a decade old now.

The woman behind him was probably no older than that scrawl. Her dress sense was simplistic, something he had seen somewhere.

Where though? Sullivan was aware of the younger woman's harsh breathing.

He tensed, remembering an incident he had heard about from one of his chess buddies.

Lower Stakk residents had been brutally attacked, a whole family killed while waiting for a faulty ascend tube that never came.

Sullivan's fingers nudged the end of his small cutter, something he had carried on the advice of a fellow resident, showing him how to modify its short range beam into a razor sharp machete, since had he heard the seemingly tall but brutal tale.

Hearing a hitch in the harsh breathing, Sullivan turned and was struck in the stomach with a thundering punch.

"Off-world filth," spat the woman, her eyes filled with loathing and disgust.

Sullivan coughed, stumbling back, staring at the thing wrapped like a sheath around her fist.

"*PummelFist*," he groaned, stunned, hand on his bruised stomach. "You're an officer... of the Security – ergh..." His head was whipped to the side, the punch blinding him. As his head was sent smashing against the keypad of the shaft, he felt his jaw crack.

He yelled brokenly in pain, falling to the floor as the girl swept a lithe leg under him.

He fell back, striking his head against the wall. Blinking back stars he looked up into the woman's snarling face.

He had no time to think, as a kick smacked into his stomach bile rose in his throat. Sullivan just reacted as fast as he could.

He pulled the cutter from his pocket, aiming at her slender leg as she aimed another kick at him. The cutter hummed into life.

But it did not reach its target. The girl moved with a speed he had only seen on holo'fights. She grabbed his wrist, breaking it, Sullivan's limp fingers dropping the still active cutter straight past his face, tracing a hot line of pain as it sliced open his cheek.

Choking and spluttering he screamed, blood and bile mixed in his senses.

Sullivan tried to pull back, put some distance between him and the mad teen. She grabbed a handful of his long hair and slammed his head viciously against the opposite wall of the shaft.

"Scum." She spat in his face, blinding his eye that was not splattered with his own blood.

She picked up the cutter as he whimpered on the floor.

Then the door opened and three figures, hazy to Sullivan, entered. He sighed in relief.

Help had arrived from his chess mates, or at best the Security Corps for true.

"Do it, Constable," said one of them. "Complete your civic duty."

The Constable glared hatefully down at injured Sullivan and slashed the cutter across his body, cutting him cleanly in half.

"Messy I suppose, but necessary," said the other.

"Only then shall they learn."

"No person is an island, but that shall change," said the last, smiling grimly.

VI

DuSalle sat at the small console desk in his new apartment in Stakk-Flat Euro One-Delta. It was better known to the residence as Anton Fellis, a famous holo' artist from the Planetary Unity days on Pelimar. DuSalle was finalising the dictation of his report to the Security Corps' interlinked database.

The Detective grimly reflected on the incidents that previous evening.

He had been revived speedily by a disgruntled Chapel.

DuSalle had said he was extremely exhausted, having been shipped over to the Eastern Quad fairly early straight after one of his duty shifts, and he had trekked half the quad to find Chapel, though it was embarrassing to DuSalle to be awoken like a trainee on his first Scuffle.

The forensics team had been hastily called to the scene. Directly before DuSalle and Chapel could ask any questions of the staff, they were ordered to immediately report to Chief Vice's office.

"So," the Quad Chief had said, his voice measured, but DuSalle had seen the veins on the man's forehead ready to explode. "I get you a new partner and then you march into the office of a very important affiliate of the Envoy Building." His voice gained a nasty edge. "Without warrant or even identifying yourselves to the secretary, who by the way is lodging a complaint. Would you care to explain any of this, Inspector?"

"Sir, may I say," Chapel had said, in an equally calm but suppressing tone, oblivious to Vice's raging, "that first I was not notified of a new partner and I could not leave an officer at a loose end, and secondly I was unaware that the man in question was dead. Had I known, I would have told the secretary of any danger to the Magistrate. As to her complaint, it is unfounded. She may simply need counselling."

Vice's jowls had then gone a livid scarlet. "He was not a mere Magistrate, Chapel, he was – was a –"

"A Stellar Sovereignty Viceroy, Inspector," a woman's voice had butted in.

"Councillor Balla –"

"Please, Chief Vice." The Beneficial government representative had waved the Chief back into the seat he had leapt from. The door of Vice's office was closed and bolted behind her as she sat on the edge of the Chief's desk. "The Benefactor has allowed my office to explain this situation to these officers and to you also. Viceroy Clove was an emissary from Sovereign Xavier himself, a negotiator, who wishes our two governments to be on a more steadfast ground."

"Councillor Unisa Balla, Shadow Foreign Office Deputy?" Chapel had mused aloud. "Aren't you in Kelly's party, the Isolationists? I'm surprised you're representing this situation."

"The Benefactor has entrusted me with this report only, Inspector, though I am fully aware of your feelings on the Isolationist front."

"As Isolationists, should you even have a front at all?" the Inspector had mused aloud again. DuSalle, despite the situation, had admired Chapel's humour.

"Inspector! Control yourself in the presence of the Councillor," Chief Vice had growled warningly.

"My apologies, Councillor. I was out of line with my remark." Chapel had inclined his head toward Balla, whose rather stern appearance had made her acknowledgement look strained to the point of distaste at accepting anything from the Inspector.

"His death is a blow, gentlemen, a deep blow to this government," she had grimaced. "We have only a matter of five days to report the death of Viceroy Clove before members of the Inner Dynastical Congress arrive. They will want answers and results." Her dark gaze had fallen heavily upon Chapel and DuSalle. "That is where you come in, gentlemen. As of tomorrow, you will begin the investigation into the murder of Viceroy Tyler Clove. You will report to either Chief Vice or myself. You will debrief any and all reasoning and, or evidence into your personal logs, which will be governmentally sealed upon submission to this office. Good day, gentlemen." She sat back slightly, but neither Chapel nor DuSalle had moved to leave.

"Sir, I do not need a partner," Chapel had said firmly. DuSalle had felt greatly put out at this comment, though his focus was on Vice.

"Sadly, Inspector," Vice, a vicious glint in his eye, had replied, "you are to work together. As you were both on the scene of the crime, this information is to not leave the office, understand? Now, go home and rest, as I'm sure you will need it for tomorrow, and don't forget to sign out under the Partner Log with the Desk Sergeant, either, Chapel. Dismissed!"

"Sir, Councillor." Chapel had bowed to the stern woman and then saluted their Chief.

Both the Inspector and DuSalle left after signing out as their new roles as Patrol Partners. With the surly but amused Desk Sergeant, Chapel offered only a customary nod of parting to DuSalle, who made his way to his locker and from there to his new flat.

Exhausted, DuSalle had filed his finished report for the end of the day, then logged off duty.

Undressing, he got into his new four poster bed, which was much softer and larger than his dorm bed, whereas usually when his head met the solid block of a pillow he was dead to the world, but this new softness kept him awake for a while longer before he found a position he was comfortable with.

VII

DuSalle felt he had only dozed off when his holo'com buzzed him awake for the morning.

He slapped the answer button, "Mushi, mushi?" the Detective said Blearily.

The transparent torso of an overtly cheery Chapel appeared above the plate.

"Good morning, Detective! I do hope you had a good night's rest as we now we have many errands to run for our new Chief, the Councillor!"

"I'll be down in fifteen minutes, Sir," said DuSalle, wearily.

"Make that ten, Detective. Those Patrol clods have been clomping all over my evidence, so I want a good look over Clove's office and his apartments. See you then!"

Nine minutes later, DuSalle met with Chapel in the carpool of the Stakk-Flat. Chapel was dressed again in the long trench coat, but underneath was a faded blue tunic with over large and frayed looking boots, more commonly used by environmental technicians outside the domes in the toxic atmosphere of Pelimar.

"Ah, Fellis," said Chapel conversationally, looking over the car pool. DuSalle was not sure if the Inspector was actually talking to him or just voicing it out generally to the air itself. "I remember his work well, all swirls and angles of interlocking structures, it is very rare to use both together in that way, except in two-dimensional artwork, but Fellis always liked to be the exception to the rule. Man after my own heart, were we allowed to be artfully inclined at all."

"Sir," said DuSalle, cautiously, feeling that the man in front of him was finally living up to those wild locker room rumours.

Chapel's long features twitched into a smirk which was gone in an instant. "Let's go, Detective. First stop – the Medical Centre's Private Morgue."

"But, Sir, I thought we were going to search his office first?" said DuSalle, confused.

Chapel gave him a hard icy look over the top of the patrol car. "Councillor Balla is not in command of this investigation, Detective. So her criteria for gathering evidence is not to be taken as noted. That message was for her benefit alone. Despite the freedom that she has given us, all mentions of us and indeed Clove, will be monitored. I've always felt that some flexibility of movement is required, don't you agree, Detective?"

"Yes Sir," said DuSalle, agreeably, to which Chapel rolled his eyes and got into the passenger seat.

"I've stored my reports from the previous missing Constable case into the car's on-board computer, which I want you to brush up on before we get to the Envoy building. Oh, yes," Chapel gestured to two paper bags by DuSalle's feet. "I bought breakfast, possibly a bit more greasy to what you're used to, but can't have you falling back on running down a suspect can I, eh?" Again the Inspector flashed the scythe-swiping-like grin at the Detective again.

"No Sir," answered DuSalle as he logged on to the console, then dug unquestionably into his bag of greasy breakfast.

***

"...So as you can see, if that hole wasn't tunnelled into his neck, he'd be totally healthy and, more importantly, live and kicking," said Unit Chief Coroner Barnis Flowynn, with total seriousness.

His white lab coat and spectacles glowing in the harsh light of his office, looked across at Chapel and DuSalle as the x–rayed holo' of the deceased Clove's body hovered above his cluttered desk.

"Corpse humour at this hour is not appreciated, Flowynn," frowned Chapel, looking at the transparent frame of the Magistrate between them. As fluxed between a detailed internal view, the man's apparent strong and stocky bone structure and then a tanned nude form. "What is your reckoning on the cause of the hole in the man's neck?"

The Coroner shifted several transparencies for a moment, his tired and worn features twisting in annoyance as he looked across his small desk. Glancing from Chapel to DuSalle, he sighed heavily.

Flowynn tapped a contact on the desk and the holo'form changed into zooming in on life sized version of Clove's head, which revolved like a living bust above the desk.

It allowed DuSalle and Chapel to study the man's face for a moment.

DuSalle thought he looked like one of those holo'flick stars, all tall, ruggedly handsome with an intense almost unfathomable look. The head turned several times before stopping where the back of the head was toward them with the small injury, a small puncture to the base of the spine, evident to them.

"Well, I've ruled out a modified laser cutter. This was not domestic or a mugging after all." He looked pointedly at both Chapel and DuSalle.

"As I said, we can only tell you the basics. Orders of Quad Chief Vice, you understand." Chapel held up his hands and shrugged in a placating manner, focusing on the desk of files strewn across it.

Flowynn sighed again, his spectacles flashing, but nodded. "Not a blaster or *PummelFist* type weapon either. My report is more detailed." The Coroner slid an info-chip over to Chapel who slipped it into an inside pocket of his large trench coat, "He'd been dead for three maybe four hours, putting his death around seventeen hundred and a quarter hours. A light drinker, judging by the state of his liver. Stomach contents and the minimal levels of vitamin supplements mark him as a vegan, used to a rich diet. Hormone stabilisers indicate several allergies, all treatable." Flowynn flicked through a number of transparencies. "Aside from the unusually small wound that had no extensive powder or burn marks –"

"Suggestive of a laser, Sir?" asked DuSalle,

"A laser of very high intensity, yes, Detective. Modular radiation suggests it was fired from five hundred feet."

"Five hundred?" exclaimed Chapel, leaning forward.

"Correct," said Flowynn, turning from the Detective to the Inspector. "The lethal range of most common laser bolts is two hundred."

"I see," replied Chapel, seeming to log that in his mind. "Fired from an angle?"

"Thirty-five degrees, I'd say." His brow furrowed again.

"Good. Continue, Flowynn."

"Fine. The victim has the usual caucuses on his hands, evidence of overuse of holo'stylus. Rather badly torn ligaments in the right thigh, an old sports injury of sorts."

"Zero gravity?"

"No, on the ground. Possibly wrestling, running or horse riding," said Flowynn, "though he was not an active sportsman, however. Mainly lots of exercise to stay fit."

"Any distinguishing marks?" asked Chapel.

"Tattoo of a dragon, seems to be have been quiet recent, on his left forearm, though the pigmentation is strange. Not sure of that. There were few other unusual factors too."

Chapel's head came up at this, his gaze completely on Flowynn. "Yes?"

"No fingerprints, not that they'd been surgically removed either. He also had no navel, again no evidence of removal. Not uncommon in clones, I suppose, but still odd, yes?"

"I suspect not, Flowynn," said Chapel, with a bored shrug. "About the tattoo, the pigmentation what was odd?"

"It contained no ink. Many tattoos are DNA bonded, but only to stop them from fading. This one, however," the Coroner's sloping shoulders twitched up and down. "Not sure if it pertains to anything, but I can run a check on it."

"That would be greatly appreciated, Flowynn. Anything else?"

"Yes. If I'm to autopsy him completely, I will need his files." He levelled Chapel with a pointed look.

"Again, I'm very sorry. Chief's orders, you see." Flowynn slumped in his chair, his spectacles glaring white, shading his eyes completely.

"This information is to be sent straight to my database, no delay, and delete the original."

Flowynn sat up straighter with indignity. "What "

"Not my orders, Coroner, Chief Vices'." The Inspector shrugged again. "Any problems with that, you can take it up with him yourself. Good day, Flowynn."

DuSalle and Chapel left Medic Squad offices. Chapel instead of DuSalle took the driving seat, though seemed in no mood to state where they were headed to next.

The Coroner's frustration seemed to permeate the recycled air in the retro-fitted patrol car as it coasted sedately through midday traffic.

Chapel stared straight ahead, taking an interest in the ID plate of the service delivery truck before them.

DuSalle was not fooled. Something about the whitening of his knuckles on the control wheel and his near silent sighs as they turned into another valley between the dome scrapers, told of his shared annoyance of this case.

However the Detective was sure it was not for the same reasons that their hands were tied with information.

VIII

Chapel directed DuSalle around Clove's office, scowling at the floor and muttering about the Forensic Squad.

"Nothing but sloppiness," the Inspector growled. "Stomping around. That lamp on the desk there was not in that position when we arrived, it's been straightened, as has the chair! Damnable idiocy!"

DuSalle stopped ruffling through the tidied pile of transparencies filed in the 'IN' tray of Clove's desk. "There was not much to move. They've taken fingerprints, DNA samples, anything that was relevant, Sir."

"There are more relevant things than DNA and finger smudges, Detective," Chapel tutted. "It is the personality of the individual that is most important, that is lost when someone else clears up after them." He moved to the walls suddenly, as if struck by an idea.

"Sir, there is one question I have wanted to ask you since we met, actually..." began DuSalle.

"How I knew your name and rank?" Chapel finished for him.

"Yes, Sir," blinked DuSalle, thinking he should be used to that by now.

"I have heard a lot of rumours of my powers of detection, Detective," said the Inspector, grimly. "Some even say I carve up bodies into minuscule pieces and dissect insects." He smiled slightly. "Even pray to primeval alien gods for guidance."

"All of which is false and total nonsense, DuSalle. When you entered the bar, I saw a man with a confident stride, like his ego had been raised by a few degrees." He held up a hand to stop DuSalle from saying anything, "but also with a few questions on his mind. I heard they were transferring someone from the Western Quads here by the name of DuSalle. There are a lot of places in the Eastern Quads I still haven't been," he shrugged, "so you could have been someone else entirely, but you have the attributes of someone from the Western Quads. Firstly, your armour is a slightly darker and less scuffed which meant it was newly issued. They do transfer very few from the Western Quads. Your tanned skin, which ends at the neck and wrist, told of time spent in the soya and rice paddies, not in enclosed spaces, in the shadow of dome scrapers. Also, your red hair and rather tall stature told of an upbringing in the plantations. There are not many redheads around city areas, not sure why that is myself," the Inspector shrugged. "Also making you not very streetwise, as I would have never stood that close when shouting at someone." DuSalle grinned sheepishly, but demurred quickly.

"As to your rank, well," the Inspector smiled sweepingly, "the pips were not all new – a rather inexpensive gesture the Security Corps has donned recently, except for one, which gleamed with an unpolished light."

"That's incredible, Sir," said DuSalle. "It sounds so simple when you say that."

"An attention to detail, Detective," said Chapel simply as he moved toward the furthest wall, rapping it with his knuckles, "which I expect to further with this case."

DuSalle stared at this odd behaviour as he took two files from the 'OUT' pile.

Chapel put his ear to the wall and started to tap at it, then with a sigh moved to another section of the wall and do the same again.

As the sun began to crest the sky, DuSalle checked the draws of the filing cabinet and the desk, Chapel moving around the room.

"Did you check the schematics of this building, DuSalle?" asked Chapel, in that annoying conversational but distracted tone. He tapped a section closer to the wall-spanning window. "If you had checked them closely you would've seen that the wall on this side of the office is a foot thicker than all the others." Chapel crouched and tapped again.

"You mean it's got some sort of hidden compartment?" frowned DuSalle, dropping the pages to help Chapel. As he did a slip of red paper fell out of the pile.

DuSalle made a grab for it as Chapel rushed to his side.

"Gloves, DuSalle, gloves," the Inspector said, thrusting a pair of blue rubber gloves at DuSalle.

The Detective snapped them on and then crouched down to pick up the slip of paper.

DuSalle held it up between them.

"They don't usually use paper, not here at least," said Chapel. "Only for a Spatial Vehicle Docket. 'East Quadrant forty-seven, signed by Dock Master Lemuel Naming, co-signed by the Captain or Pilot of the *Silver Frame*' it says here." Chapel started to dig into the pockets of his vast coat, finally pulling out a small plastic baggie.

"What do you think this is?" asked DuSalle, as he dropped it into the proffered container.

"The date on this recite corresponds with the arrival of Clove, DuSalle," said Chapel, his eyes suddenly alight with something that DuSalle could not yet fathom. "What we have here, is a possible entry point into opening up this case."

"So this SVD thing is important how, Sir?"

"The Spatial Vehicle Docket is a claim," said Chapel. "A recite on your ship, an insurance and so forth; the docket is given to crew and passengers, enabling a tracking on unclaimed items and possessions."

"So this SVD thing is important how, exactly?"

"They said Clove was only here for a short time, yes?" DuSalle nodded. "All governmental and administrative officials have always been given housing, whether it is in the form of a hotel or rented lodgings, but always a place to stay. Each Docking Bay has a different hostel or rental procedure for such officials, with this SVD being in a high rent area. Quad forty-seven has only one of these locales." He grinned openly, though DuSalle still did not see the significance of this find.

Chapel started pacing deep in thought. DuSalle stepped back, the sun glinting high over his broad shoulders.

Chapel muttered to himself, "Yes, yes, this is it. Finally a break!" he whirled on the Detective. "This case has put me to the test indeed, my vision being twenty-twenty, but on this case it has been only five-by-fi –" Suddenly he stopped, looking over DuSalle's shoulder.

"Hello, what have we here?" He moved DuSalle out of the way with a thin but unexpectedly strong hand.

DuSalle watched the Inspector, as his gaze was far and away out of the window. Again he rifled through his pockets and produced the most strangest device the Detective had ever seen.

A rather bulky mess of wires was set atop what looked like a former gear shifter from a Trike-Pod, the transport for most of the older citizenry, but nestled with the wiring was miniature hologram plate and a circle of glass.

Chapel made a couple of adjustments fiddling with a small volume dial from a portable holo'set on the handle. The plate glowed and an image appeared above it.

DuSalle realised he was looking at a magnified view of the window, or rather the three inch thick plate glass.

"As I said, DuSalle," said Chapel over his shoulder, as the Detective stepped closer, "my eyesight is twenty-twenty." He nodded towards the image, which had blown up the section of glass that Chapel had his device trained on. "That is a visible distortion in the glass."

DuSalle frowned. "But I don't understand, Sir. What has it to do with us if the glass was fitted with a warp in it?"

Chapel sighed. "Think, Detective, think! This glass was machine made. If there had been a warp in it, would it have made it off the production line?" He raised an eyebrow questioningly.

DuSalle shook his head.

"This, DuSalle, is the work of a unique and terrible weapon," Chapel said, visibly excited. "Something that tells us two things. One – that this murder was committed from a distance and by someone of incredibly accurate skill."

Dazed, DuSalle mechanically asked the obvious.

"The second," replied Chapel, his smile gone but the fire still in his eyes, "is that the murderer was sitting at the window of the Envoy's very own rented apartments!"

IX

The short plump building stood on the edges of the Chandler City's Beneficial government grounds. Close by were dome-scraping Stakk-Flat apartments, which housed several hundred administrative staff, who swarmed the grand Chamber of Patrons.

For various security and official reasons, these imposing and important letting structures were spaced out in such a way to deter anti-government attacks.

One of these specialised Stakk-Flats stood out from the rest as it was closer to the slope of the massive eco-dome but eclipsed by the massive forest wall.

Before the Reconsolidation with the rest of the galaxy, these buildings were merely for the party officials to be close to their destinations, but with contact being made with the Stellar Sovereignty and the Pastoral Regions, who were held in a shaky truce, they were used to house visiting officials due to the increased number of letting agencies, various rental agreements were made with several volunteer families or agents of the government to house the less frequent visitors to the neutral planet.

"Thank you, Mrs. Tuvel. It has been a long time since anyone asked so nicely to see my credentials."

It was here that DuSalle found himself in the pristinely carpeted hallway of Stakk-Flat 542, nicknamed Tiberius Rankle. It was named after the first colonist to convert many of the former colonial ships into housing for the growing populace.

The Detective was studying the holo's of a young married couple and their long line of relatives along the walls.

"Now, can you describe the resident's habits?" asked Chapel.

"Yes. He was always clean and tidy, always polite and always on time with the rent," said the middle-aged landlady.

Her dark eyes were twitching around her pristine hallway, never looking directly at either of them.

"Was there anything unusual about him, Mrs. Tuvel?" asked DuSalle.

"Well, there was nothing much to tell." Her face screwed up for a second. DuSalle thought it a bit of a performance, but Chapel was patient. "Oh, yes… yes, I remember now. I think he had a tattoo on his arm. I saw it when… well I saw it." She muttered, "a dragon I think it was."

"I see," said Chapel, cutting across DuSalle before he could say anything. "What were his clothes like? Did he dress well?"

At that, Mrs. Ervya Tuvel's semi-botoxed cheek twitched. "Clothes?"

"Yes, Mrs. Tuvel," said Chapel, patiently. "Was he shabby or smartly dressed?"

"Oh, well Ben – I mean Mr. Kelly – was always smartly dressed."

"What –"

"Do not interrupt, Detective," said Chapel, sharply.

Silenced, DuSalle caught a look of something pass over Chapel's face, though it was gone in an instant.

"Thank you, Mrs. Tuvel," he said. "May we have a look in his rooms?"

"Yes, yes of course." She flushed slightly and gave over the key card. "I have the original. I give a copy to the tenants, though I haven't been up there in a while."

"I'm sure that you haven't," said Chapel smiling. The landlady's face flushed again. "Thank you again, Mrs. Tuvel."

The landlady stepped reluctantly aside as the two Security Corps officers went up the short landing to the rented room.

With a small cot in one corner and a low plastic table beside it, the only feature of the room seemed to be a large chest of drawers and a small bookcase in the opposite corner.

"Mmph!" said Chapel, looking at the clean and bare looking bedroom. "So cleaning strikes again! Interesting arrangement though."

"Shouldn't we have gotten a warrant?" asked DuSalle, the thought suddenly occurring to him.

"Not in this case, Detective," said Chapel, a small frown on his face as he looked about the room. DuSalle felt a little put out by the Inspector's casual dismissal. "After all, I only wanted a cursory look and also, it seems Mrs. Tuvel, would be a little reluctant to ask for any legal documentation at this stage."

"You mean she's sleeping with her tenants?" DuSalle frowned, a little disgusted.

"Possibly, or just peeping on them." Chapel shrugged, eyes still scanning the room. "An assassin could have been here, DuSalle. Could have followed Clove, watched him as lived here at any rate." He looked in a few drawers and even under the bed, but found nothing of interest to him.

As DuSalle looked around, he thought it was time to speak of what he was truly thinking.

"Did she say Ben Kelly?"

"That she did, Detective," said the Inspector. He ran a finger across the windowsill, then clapped his hands together to rid himself of the dust. "The infamous Ben Kelly, direct descendant of Kurt Mully, the second Benefactor of the city. I wondered if he would really use his name. Even though these are specialised tenements, she doesn't seem to be up to date with recent political news, though she does seem overly fond of her tenant, nonetheless."

"But…"

"No, Detective, it's not him," said Chapel, turning and looking at him sternly. "A poor joke, certainly for Balla and the Benefactor, but still far too obvious. Agreed?"

"Right, Sir." Rather dejectedly and avoiding Chapel's amused glance, DuSalle started poking around in the chest of drawers by the bed, finding nothing.

"Although, it could have been a double bluff," said Chapel thoughtfully. "This place seems far too public, but still, I heard news a while back."

"You mean Kelly ejected from the Chamber of Patrons, Sir?"

Chapel nodded, as DuSalle had heard the story on his own Narro-Caster the night before. "For a violent outburst or something, wasn't it, Sir?"

"Correct, Detective, but that was a few weeks ago." Chapel frowned. "The ability to disguise and hide from detection is not simple. With surveillance, ID cards and DNA signatures being only a small part of our tracking system – once one knows how it all works, even then. But for a double bluff such as this? Using his contacts to discover this? Then attacking the man from his own window?" Chapel sucked in a breath between his teeth. "Harder still to contemplate, DuSalle, is that it goes against the use of the weapon. Kelly was a staunch supporter of independence and isolation from the rest of the galaxy. This was a well thought out plan. He would not use a weapon of unknown type."

"Since we know nothing of it, then it could have been designed here, Sir," said DuSalle, reasonably. "Kelly and his group may have designed it. Making it home grown, therefore useable against off-worlders, Sir."

"Possible, possible," muttered Chapel, looking around the small room, turning over transparencies scattered on the desk beside the tiny porthole-like window.

"What about the tattoo, Sir?"

"From the look of it, it resembles the same artistry of La Flayed Dragon's neon graphic, DuSalle." Chapel continued to move about the room, lifting the touch lamp off the bed-side table, checking it over. "He dined there on various occasions."

"So what? It's a memento or something then?"

"Possible again, DuSalle, though of the Flayed Dragon?" Chapel shrugged again, though looked more thoughtful this time. "Though it would discount Kelly, he was not a man to get tattoos. If Clove is here in secret, why use such a public or controversial figure?"

"No idea, Sir," said DuSalle, completely stumped.

DuSalle half turned away from the contemplating Inspector when something caught his attention.

A small slip of plastic-parchment which had caught his eye was poking out from underneath a battered looking pseudo–pine chest of draws.

He bent down and reached for it but it slipped into the small gap at the bottom.

"Sir, could you help me with this?" said DuSalle, lifting one side of the chest of drawers with difficulty. Chapel leapt forward eagerly and helped the Detective move back the chest of drawers, DuSalle straightened and looked over the plastic-parchment. "What do you think it is, Sir?"

"Off hand, these numbers appear to be a notation of some kind," said Chapel, turning the paper between his thin fingers. "Not a code, no. Not at least a kind for a message, at any rate. As they are arranged differently, that I'm sure of." The Inspector looked over to the window and ran up to it, looking at the plastic slip again.

DuSalle watched him as he raised his head to look out the window and then back to the paper several times.

"Co-ordinates, Detective, positions of windows. Look." Chapel pointed out the window, as DuSalle joined him at the windowsill. "Seven up, four in and one down." He was now pointing out of the window to the office of Tyler Clove.

"But then the murder was done from here, like you said," exclaimed DuSalle, delighted and amazed.

"Possible again, Detective," said Chapel doubtfully. "Or maybe we're meant to think it was. I don't believe that the killer could have been here. That would be too easy."

"But who would set up something like this, even knowing that it might fail?"

"Someone who knows what this means, DuSalle, for this planet and for who is surrounding it."

As DuSalle was left to ponder this statement, he followed Chapel out of the room. Again they met with Mrs. Tuvel in the corridor of her apartment.

"Here is the key card," said Chapel returning it to the landlady, "and may I add, Mr. Tuvel may also need to be questioned if he is around."

"He wasn't around, he never is, that's…" said Mrs. Tuvel harshly, her face pouting as her eyes went wide, as though she had said too much.

"I see," said Chapel, slowly. "Next time you have a tenant Mrs. Tuvel, make sure you know him well before letting him into your bed." He levelled a cold stare at the gaping woman, as DuSalle gaped also. "Goodbye, Mrs. Tuvel."

With a furious red-faced glare before DuSalle was even halfway through the doorway, Mrs. Tuvel abruptly closed the door on them.

"That went well, don't you think, Detective?" said Chapel, with a grin.

X

"So what do we know, Detective?" asked Chapel, abruptly pulling the patrol car up into a higher lane of traffic, causing DuSalle to fumble with the plastic baggie which he was idly examining.

"Well, Sir," he started after a pause, looking forward. As they passed through the vast canyons of towering Stakk–Flats, Chapel was in his peripheral vision, slumped slightly over the steering wheel, also seeming to stare intently ahead. "Firstly we have Clove, murdered in his office, but not from his office. The assassin achieved his or her goal from a distance, with a weapon of undisclosed…"

"Let us not speak about the assassin, his weapon or weapons of choice, or who it might be," said Chapel, dismissively. "Clove and his movements are of a deeper import, as it was those movements that probably got him killed."

DuSalle mentally shuffled through the data they had received from Chief Vice.

"When he arrived, Sir, he was giving lodgings with the more than amiable Mrs. Tuvel…"

" 'When he arrived', a good phrasing, Detective. A simple collection of words to display in front of complete unimportant nonsense," the Inspector huffed. "His travel and arrival to this city is of far more of interest than any of his movements afterwards." Chapel scowled out of the window, "No doubt it will be hard to track such things, without the correct procedures, protocols and such." He breathed out gruffly.

DuSalle stared dumbstruck at the Inspector.

As he had heard all the rumours of Jase Chapel, even from the graffiti in the toilets of his Bunk House in Training School, he knew just about all there was to know about 'Bloodhound' Chapel.

Said to be a man of colossal ego, so caught up in the petty dealings of the citizenry rather than solving the seemingly easy looking crimes, going about testing and collating every piece of insignificant evidence in finest detail of a deranged fanatic.

DuSalle had often imagined Chapel as a zealous robed figure with blood-stained face and a wide grimace of glee splitting his features as he toiled over stretched out entrails of a gutted Quazian or Ai'tol in some shadowy chamber of horrors.

This Chapel, however, who sat across from the Detective, appeared to be much more than that. He was truly frustrated and angry at the system he was a part of, with completely no shred of guilt in what he did.

Though it was not that far from DuSalle's image of the man, the Detective had seen one thing which officers of the Corps seemed not to believe or allow; the one thing that would, in due course, land the Inspector in the Interrogator's chair in the bowels of the IJ Section.

Passion, a passion for solving, investigating and ultimately eliminating all sources of crime, single handed.

Officers of the Security Corps were forbidden from emotion.

In fact it was far more than to do with sensual and primal temperament, but the pursuit of investigations were possibly not considered in the same realm as anything of a sexual nature.

The reasons that Chapel was an Inspector was to do with his aptitude to out think and out do the criminals, after all, not still ranked as a Constable and forever overlooked, as DuSalle himself had once been.

"So you think we should start with the Docking Bays then, Sir?" asked DuSalle, after only a moment of silence.

Chapel brought them up to an intersection of traffic where a red blur sped past them.

Seconds later, it was followed by the familiar whirling grey haze of a Security Corps patrol car.

"Sir! What are you doing?" exclaimed DuSalle, as Chapel pulled around to pursue the chasing patrol car.

"I thought that was perfectly obvious, Detective," said Chapel.

"But, Sir, we are on assignment!" protested the Detective, as they linked up into the fast lane of traffic. "We can't..."

"DuSalle, I see it is going to take an extraordinary amount of time for you to except that I do not see in restricted and straight lanes, such as this fellow we are tailing." Chapel grimaced as a wedge-like neon-blue Strato-Trekker beeped her annoyance from behind them as they joined the flow of speeding traffic. "Now, if you're done questioning me, get the lead patrol car on the horn so they know that they have company."

"Get them on the what, Sir?" exclaimed DuSalle again.

"The radio, Detective, the radio!"

DuSalle picked up the handset off the dash and clicked the contact.

"This is Pat seven-niner-four, patch Beta-Alpha two," he looked ahead at the front patrol car's number plate, "to Pat two-zero-five, over."

"What?" said Chapel suddenly, rounding on DuSalle. "What was that number?"

"Two-zero-five, Sir," said DuSalle promptly.

"Oh, damn it, it's them," growled Chapel, thumping the steering wheel. "Why can't I get away from them?"

Just as Chapel was done grumbling, a gravely and faintly amused voice spilled over the loudspeakers.

"Hullo there, Inspector," said the lead patrol car from the speakers. "Nice of you to join our little convoy, though it's gratuitous even for you, Sir."

"Sergeant Wane, please keep Constable Brig in line," said Chapel smoothly, taking the handset from DuSalle.

There was a brief sharp crackle of noise, which may or may not have been someone swearing, but then another voice came over the speakers.

"Inspector, we are glad to have your assistance, though it may be seen as over kill," said a smooth, though lisping high voice of a Ai'tolian, "as we both have our own assignments to be found, do we not?"

Chapel glared at the handset. "You were assigned to the Warren case! Without my consultation!" he exclaimed heatedly, his face contorted in pure rage for a moment.

Just as DuSalle thought the Inspector was about to truly explode, something strange seemed to wash over him. His fists were no longer clamped to the handset or the steering column and his features were again near smugly serene.

It was as though Chapel had had a mental cold shower all in a matter of seconds.

"Well, I suppose my workload was a little hefty, Sergeant," he said, his eyes narrowing at the patrol car in front of them. "Thank you for taking on such a task."

"We're able to take this monkey, Inspector," replied Brig carelessly, "so thanks, but no thanks, Sir."

"I am senior officer here, Sergeant," said Chapel, frostily again, "so if anyone will be in charge, it will be I. Got that?"

"Yes, Sir," said Brig and Wane, with a hint of steel in their voices.

DuSalle forced himself to focus on red the pod in front of them, as they came up to the other patrol car's side. This was serious business. The questions now bubbling forcefully in the Detective's mind could wait for now.

"The speedometer reading is very unusual, Detective," said Chapel, looking at the display on the snub nosed gun-like device strapped to the dashboard. "The Trans-Comm. traffic grid has a leeway of ten miles per hour over or under the limit, giving the public an illusion of free choice," he said, somewhat disgusted, though DuSalle had known this perfectly well and applauded its use. "This vehicle is somehow far exceeding it."

"That's impossible, Sir. Even we can't exceed that limiter," exclaimed DuSalle, as the red pod seemed to drift further away from them even though they had reached maximum speed and now would been issued with a driving offence.

"We need to swap over, DuSalle."

"What, Sir?" said the Detective alarmed, as Chapel quickly unbuckled his safety harness.

"We need to stop him and I can't do that with my hands tied to the controls, can I, Detective?"

"Right, Sir," said DuSalle, less confidently as he pulled at his own harness.

Awkwardly they crossed over. As DuSalle grabbed the controls and settled himself into the driving seat, Chapel simply threw himself into the passenger side and pulled open the glove box, several bits of equipment tumbling out.

The Inspector sorted through the pile of wires and bits of circuit boards, creating a wrapped up bundle.

"I told Vice I would not do this again," sighed Chapel, glaring at the red pod in front of them as it swerved into the next intersection of traffic, almost crashing into the granite wall of a Stakk-Flat, which DuSalle managed to deftly avoid along with the other patrol car. "But I suppose this is urgent." He unrolled the bundle onto his lap. "And Vice has been known to forgive such minor things as hacking," to reveal a touch type keypad terminal, "in the past which were explainable," with a small holo' plate insert on the top.

Pulling out a wire from the terminal he attached the plug into the radio interface. The holo' plate glowed and columns of letters and numbers resolved into the Trans-Comm. Tower's Traffic System grid.

"Sir, you can't!"

"Watch the road, Detective!" cried back Chapel.

DuSalle turned and automatically swerved the patrol car to the left, just a large flat object flew passed them.

"They're throwing things at us!" shouted DuSalle in amazement.

"Damn!" said Chapel. "I thought they'd find me, but not that soon. We'll have to back track! Use the TERBs subsystems." His deft fingers flew over the keyboard. The lines of numbers were replaced by a grid of interconnecting lines, as it went through the thousands of sensors in the walls of the Stakk-Flats of Traffic Examination and Research Beacons. "There that's us – oh, hello, yes I'm legally illegal, yes, yes – let's get a bit closer to our quarry shall we, DuSalle? Yes, here we are."

Suddenly the patrol car jolted forward, crushing DuSalle back into the driver's seat. Chapel crowed with delight as the screen flashed up a warning in glowing red letters. They overtook Brig and Wane who shouted furiously over the radio.

As they were now catching up to the pod which was still speeding away in front of them.

"Now to slow you down!" Chapel exclaimed, his fingers working at top speed again.

DuSalle could now feel the buffeting speed of the patrol car, as control had been given solely to the driver, rather than the restraining guide of the Trans-Comm Tower.

He struggled with the steering wheel, trying to keep in a straight line. As they passed through heavy traffic, above and below them, it was clear that the pod in front of them had no such concerns to the welfare others, scraping past several silver teardrop Chequered-Commuters, and bouncing between two blue resin styled Stop-Stars.

"He's jamming me," exclaimed Chapel, as he typed furiously. "I've got him, DuSalle. Locked into the Traffic Net. We'll have to bring him into the fast lane."

"To street level then," muttered DuSalle, agreeing. Suddenly he swerved the patrol car as something big blurred passed them.

"Careful, don't smack into any walls now, DuSalle," said Chapel, not looking up. "I've got his ID now. He was trying to jam me, but I got in through another subsystem. I've given command over to the Controllers, as I've alerted them to the breach in their net."

DuSalle watched as from the passenger side, which apparently now had no door, something else was being shifted to the gap in the pod.

"Sir, they're throwing out their haul," said DuSalle, as wind buffeted them, dragging them both closer to a bulk freighter of Coco Chips Reserve.

"Oh, well I can't have that!" said Chapel. "Follow them closely, Detective."

Tensing, DuSalle did as ordered.

The large and bulky object flew out of the passenger side. DuSalle dodged the flying object, though it managed to clip the side of the patrol car. With a wretch DuSalle pulled the car away mere inches from hitting the side of the bulk freighter. The propulsion coils screamed in protest as he attempted to bring them down into the fast lane.

Ahead of them the red pod dropped into the line of three hundred and fifty mile-an-hour traffic.

DuSalle, quickly following behind, brought them down, with a bump across a lime Solar Jauntier. The driver looking enraged from out of his dented and scraped carapace as

DuSalle shot him a speedy apologetic glance through the side window.

Chapel looked up from keyboard. "Ah, good, now." He reached over for hand set to the radio. He tapped into the resident com channels. "Operator, link me to resident traverse, number twelve-dash-omega-one-seven on the fast lane, please."

"Connecting," stated a monotone voice.

There was a click, then Chapel said coolly into the receiver, "This is Inspector Chapel to whomever is driving the Status 4 – Solar Ennui. If you do not descend to Ground Level on the next exit, your license will not only be revoked with a hefty fine but you will also be facing charges of criminal damage, illicit hacking of government property and public expenses from the City Bursary, notwithstanding the charges of theft. Understood? This is your only warning. Inspector Chapel, out."

"Sir, you don't actually think they'll –"

"Just watch, Detective," said Chapel.

Despite his surprise, DuSalle sighed with relief as the pod did indeed take the exit, but gripped the steering wheel in alarm as the second patrol car flashed passed them, straight after it, buffeting them in the heavy and close by traffic.

"Get going then, Detective," said Chapel, his jaw set.

They caught up with the second patrol car just as it converted to street travel and slammed the now beached red pod into a massive pile of rubbish which was strewn over the alleyway.

As DuSalle landed more gently, Chapel unbuckled his harness and sprung out of the patrol car, just as the criminals clambered out of the half smashed vehicle, attempting to make a run for it.

Brig and Wane had stepped out of their patrol car and stopped the two from going any further with a warning shot from their *PummelFist* weapons, the criminals falling to the ground to avoid the bolts sizzling past their heads.

DuSalle got out and raced after Chapel, who began yelling at the two menacing looking officers as they towered over the quivering forms on the floor.

"Stop right there!" yelled Chapel again. The short Ai'tolian of the rather brutal looking pair turned. He was about to aim a kick at the one of the criminal's heads.

The Ai'tolians had been a part of the innovative Planetary Union, along with several other humanoid and non-humanoid races, which had collapsed so long ago. They had also joined, along with a smaller group of Drylians and Quazians in on the project to traverse their own star systems and colonise distant worlds, such as Pelimar and others.

After a thousand years away from the bloody trials of the massive Great Astral Expansion, the four races had co–habituated and to a certain extent also interbred, causing the usually calm and innocent Ai'tolians and even a few Quazians, with their racial subconscious psychic link, to act more brutally or irrationally than ever before.

DuSalle had met many Ai'tolians in his assignments in the West Quads. Most had been advocates of the Appointed Basilica, a small group within the formerly brutal race who now prayed to the gods of science, logic and reason. Nothing like this Sergeant Wane, currently stowing his long-toed boot into the chest of the long haired passenger.

The two officers stopped their truncheons in the middle of a second swing. The human officer, DuSalle saw by the pips on his uniform, was a Constable.

"Yeah?" said the Constable, turning to face them, as DuSalle also exited the car. "What yer want?"

"Are they armed, Sergeant?" asked Chapel, stepping up to the pair.

"No," said Wane flatly. He glared at Chapel, his vast pitiless black eyes glinting as DuSalle joined them.

"Were they attempting to attack you in anyway, Constable?" asked Chapel, turning on Brig.

"No," said the tall patrolman impassively.

"Then why were you beating them?" said Chapel. "What was the purpose, Sergeant? Before he decides to run DuSalle, cuff him will you?" he added as the criminal near Wane's foot began to get slowly to his feet.

"We were well within the legal limits of…"

"Of what? Brutality!" interjected Chapel harshly. "And that's Inspector Chapel, if you please, Constable," he added sternly. "I at least adhere to rank."

"Only when it suits, Sir," the Sergeant almost spat. "These criminals don't respect the order of things 'ere."

"So this is how they are taught," scowled Chapel, "by beatings. The legal limits you spoke of have needed changing the week after they were implemented, Sergeant. The city is not as unruly as the Directorate think. In some bizarre cases the criminals actually like being beaten so it serves no logical…"

"I don't need a lecture on street ethics, especially from you–"

"Quiet all right, Sergeant," said Chapel, cutting into their rant. He was suddenly pleasant once more. "Let us just give each other a speeding ticket, and we'll be on our way, shall we?"

The Sergeant paused, then still scowling, said, "Yes, Sir."

They wrote each other tickets, the Sergeant making out another for the criminal that was now sat in the back of their patrol car. Chapel had decided to give them the collar, as 'a peace offering' he called it. Even a boot knife could not have cut the tension in the air when he had uttered that comment.

As the Sergeant and the Inspector filled out the complicated little forms from Brig's stack in his glove compartment, the Constable, his lantern-jawed features set in that hard way of the Street Section, his pale face and sunken eyes making him look as if he'd not slept well with his many nights of patrols, sidled up to DuSalle.

"You're his new partner then, Detective," he said in a half whisper, sending a fleeting look over his shoulder at the other pair bent over the hood of Wane's patrol car.

"Yeah," said DuSalle, frowning slightly. "Didn't mean to get in your way."

"That's fine, Sir," said Brig, shrugging and adjusting his grey peaked cap uneasily. "It's just that Chapel, gotta watch 'im, he's had partners 'fore, most on hospital leave. Two are dead." DuSalle jaw must of dropped because Brig smirked. "'Fore he was in Street, Sir, he was IJ, a 'Cadre Interro' as they called 'em. Didn't know that, yeah?" said Brig, looking DuSalle in the eye, as he shook his head. "That's the reason he gets his perks, Sir. Nothin' else. They indulge the Internal Judicial Section, see? Have done since Hackett turned it around, much good it did 'im. The Inspector has links everywhere they say, Sir. Though it doesn't save those dat partner up with 'im, do it?" Brig grinned again, his perfect teeth glinting.

Then the Constable turned serious, face to face with the stunned DuSalle. "Careful how you tread, Sir, he's a slippery one is Chapel. Clever yeah, but too clever, get me, Sir?"

With that, Brig turned on his heel and left DuSalle standing there.

A call over the radio informed them to report to Vice's office. DuSalle had been afraid of this since the Inspector had instructed him to chase the criminal. This would be a black mark for sure this time. The Detective had barely been promoted and had been hauled into the office for a second time in a matter of days. No good could come of that for his record.

"You can drive this time, I think," said Chapel, as though DuSalle could refuse, watching Brig and Wane's patrol car lift off into the traffic. "I cannot abide unnecessary violence, DuSalle. More and more officers of the Security Corps seemed to be taking pleasure out of the mindless violence that a law allows. 'To Service and Preserve Order'. Pah! That should have been changed the moment it was uttered! Though few will listen to the view of one man." He took a deep breath, seeming to shake off something. "Let's get Vice's grilling out the way shall we?"

"Yes, Inspector," said DuSalle listlessly.

XI

Chief Vice was on vicious verbal form when both Chapel and DuSalle entered his office. The volume of his voice made the desk lamp vibrate as he berated Chapel on his unethical and unlawful tampering of City property. Chapel remained blithely unconcerned and explained the situation calmly.

DuSalle was surprised that Vice did not pass out from the amount of blood that was turning his tanned features almost prune-like.

Throughout the tirade, Councillor Balla stood silently aside, but not simply into space. Her dark honey eyes were zeroed straight on DuSalle.

The Detective shifted easily, feeling as if he was back at Training School and being asked a rather complex tactical question, but Balla was eyeing him in a different way – a way no one had looked at him before.

"I ought to have you both arrested, right now," said Chief Vice in a heated but formal tone of voice, which snapped DuSalle out of the hypnotic gaze. Balla broke the look to snatch up the lamp.

"But I won't," said Vice, as though sensing Balla bristling. "Not because of this case, but because you got a result and have not endangered the case to outside knowledge. Your report was rather sparse, however. I want movement on this, suspects, interviews and results on both."

"Let him speak, Chief," said Balla amicably.

Chapel spared the Councillor a brief though not entirely gracious glance as he addressed Vice.

"We have several leads, one being Cobble Industries, as Clove's arrival was through one of their ships."

"That's correct," said Balla, nodding. "The new Managing President, Simon Poper, was given the passenger, it seemed the best way."

"Yes, I would like to speak to him. Possibly Ben Kelly and the Docking Master, also."

"What?" asked Balla, startled.

"Oh, yes," said Chapel, turning to face her. "The murderer used an alias – Ben Kelly. I wished to speak with him in case he had had any dealings with Clove, which instigated him using the name, but I'm interested in the transport that is a good start and also his movements, maybe even bringing in his landlady for more formal questioning." He looked at both Vice and Balla, swinging from one to the other.

The air seemed to escape from Vice's indignant balloon as Balla nodded solemnly. "That would indeed be a good start, Inspector. You have not much time. You have complete autonomy to see this through, but not at the expense of all citizens. That is why you were called here," said Balla, glancing at DuSalle again.

"Yes, of course, Councillor," said the Inspector, inclining his head toward her respectfully.

"You will make official recordings and data input, gentlemen," said Vice, looking gravely at Chapel. "I expect this especially from you from now on, Chapel. You have your 'corder with you?" he asked, referring to the small handheld card slot recorder that was used in on the spot questioning and formal interrogations by the majority of Street Section.

"Oh yes, Sir, here it is." He fished into a deep pocket and produced it, waving it over enthusiastically in front of them like a show-and-tell in infant class.

Vice frowned at him, but curiously the Councillor smiled warmly, strangely indulgent.

"All right," said Vice, clapping his leathery palms together decisively. "I'll get the papers signed up. Meanwhile I want you to get to your reports. No slacking, either of you. This is the last time I want you in my office without more than substantial results. Understand? Dismissed!"

XII

DuSalle was surprised by how small and understated the Cobble Industries complex was. As a multi-planetary company that spanned both the Stellar Sovereignty and the Pastoral regions, the Detective thought it would be vast and grand structure, but it seemed to be huddled amongst the taller merchant and trading buildings, with the large billboard hologram logo of the interlocked C and I standing out proudly on its stunted framework being the only significant feature, like the small boy wanting in on the big boy's gang.

Director President of the Pelimar chair of Chandler City, was Simon Poper. He was heir to the Reinhart trillions, shrewd businessman of the Bass Family Plutonium Insolvency, and now a leading entrepreneur and noted contributor to various resident charities in Chandler City.

"I don't get it, Sir," said DuSalle. "How can a man like Poper be involved in such shady deals?"

"Exactly why he is, Detective," replied Chapel, as they landed on the roof of the building. "What better guise than that? A good reputation is quickly sullied if you dig deep enough, and Poper's past is only slightly shady. If it were totally clean, I would be in doubt of his character completely."

"So, as it stands, he's only a suspect in this, Sir?"

"As is stands, DuSalle, as it stands," nodded the Inspector, watching as double doors opened in front of them. "Keep your eyes open, Detective, and don't fall asleep."

"Sir," replied DuSalle stiffly as they exited the patrol car.

The entranceway into the main lobby opened as they got out. Two figures moved into the afternoon sunlight. DuSalle recognised the taller of the two, dressed in a grey kimono detailed with black dragons and lotus flowers, his black hair held by a red band in a top knot, his thin almost gaunt features stretched into an uncommon smile of greeting, while the redheaded woman beside him seemed a little more severe looking, she was dressed in a pale green executive suit, and had a white-knuckle grip on a info-pad and holo-stylus.

"Greetings, Inspector, Constable… excuse me Detective," said Simon Poper, smiling warmly. His dark eyes sparkled as he bowed low to them both. DuSalle tried hard no to show his confusion. "I hear you wish to discuss my business arrangements with your government."

Both DuSalle and Chapel returned the bow. "That is correct, Sir," said Chapel.

"Please, no formalities. I have no title of that sort, Inspector."

"Mr. Poper then."

"Yes," said Poper, "that will do nicely. This is my P.A., Miss Kathryn Pierce."

"Pierce, as in the medal winner of Truffet Dojo's Syndicate Bereavement Charity match last month?"

"Yes, that's correct," said the woman stiffly. "It was an interesting bout."

"That it was," said Chapel. "Was very challenging since they added the zero-G element, but you seemed to be born to it."

"Thank you." Pierce's stunned expression seemed to fade almost at once, as she continued, stiff again. "This way, gentlemen."

Poper was smiling amusedly as he led them into the CI building. "Yes, would you care to illuminate me as to what this is all about?"

"Of course, Mr. Poper," said Chapel, as they followed him and Pierce through the spacious grey. "We are currently investigating the death of Magistrate Tyler Clove. I believe you received the order to not broadcast this?"

"Yes, of course, Inspector," said Poper, smiling, as Pierce pressed the button for a descend shaft. "Though I have been through intense diplomatic issues before, this is a different deal, though I know the protocols."

"Ah, yes, the Reinhart inheritance," said Chapel.

"Mr. Poper has been instructed by his lawyers Duke and Raoul to not answer questions based prior to his arrival to Pelimar, Inspector," interjected Pierce. "I assumed you knew this."

"We were told that you would cooperate, Mr Poper," said Chapel, ignoring Pierce.

Poper smiled levelly at the Inspector. "I think that was an unavoidable remark, Kathryn." His eyes flicked between his PA and Chapel. "That is still a sticking point for my adoptive family, though they have disowned me through the courts. Sir Gettle was a kind man, having many children of his own and also adopting many more. My hope is that I can live up to that reputation. Your reputation, Inspector, precedes you well." He looked at DuSalle. "And this is your newest partner?"

DuSalle stood straighter as Poper had not offered to shake his hand. "Correct, Detective DuSalle." Poper and DuSalle exchanged a nod. "Your reputation precedes you also, Managing President."

Poper and Chapel stared at each other, seeming to size each other up.

"Is shipping the only industry Cobble Industries is involved in, Mr. Poper?" asked DuSalle, hoping to break the tension.

"Ah, no," said Poper, severing his stare from Chapel. "No that is not all we do here."

The ascend shaft pinged and opened onto a long corridor. "Follow me, gentlemen," said Pierce, as she led them toward double doors elaborately carved with dragons and lotus flowers, much like Poper's kimono, at the end of the corridor.

"We have many subsidiary companies under our wings. Though CI is known for its premiere import and export services, we also dabble in manufacture and pharmaceuticals, as well as media and communications," said Poper, his eyes focused on Chapel, "including various charity and public works, which are a breath of fresh air on occasion. A few theoretical redevelopment projects, as well as several personal protection and anti-theft devices are being developed by my pet company PROTech, along with a few commercial government contracts – as you know of course, Inspector."

They entered Poper's office. DuSalle had to admit it was much more impressive than any office he had been in before.

Glass display cabinets lined both sides of the office, filled with ornaments and trinkets, pre-Sovereignty and probably even pre-Unity, with a holograph work of art, above each, backed by a large window with the blank view of the bulging dome-scraper, that tower of the CI building opposite. In the centre of the room was a large ornate desk, with a faux-leather wing backed chair facing them on one side with a pair of wire frame hard chairs on the other.

"Interesting desk, Mr. Poper," said Chapel. "Imported?"

"Yes, from my native trappings on Nul'ern."

"Native? I was told you were born…"

"That…" began Kathryn. Poper raised his hand to stop her, as he turned to sit on the edge of his desk.

"No, the Inspector is quite right, Kathryn," Poper smiled. "Nul'ern is not my native system, very astute again, Inspector." Poper studied Chapel. "The location of my birth was in the Reinhart vaults. When I was awarded various parts of his estate, that was not included, though I discovered it anyway," the Managing Director of Cobble Industries shrugged. "I am told all reference to myself were destroyed by his angered relatives." He sighed, smiling slightly. "But I have spent half my life there, so it seems like home to me."

"Very good, Mr. Poper," said Chapel, inclining his head toward the Managing President. "You have been here three months, correct?"

"That is correct, Inspector," said Poper. "Now I am a very busy man. This business is…"

"A lot to take on," said Chapel, cut in, "in light of such a tragic event, Mr. Poper."

"Yes, my predecessor, Miss Te'zynn's passing was indeed terrible and shocking to many, yes," said Poper, sadly. "She was very successful here. They decided it was the pressure," Poper frowned. "I was drafted in as merely a temporary replacement, but the shareholders seemed to like my proposals, so made my appointment permanent."

"This is procedure, I'm afraid, Mr. Poper, but may I ask where you were on the night in question?"

"Night, Inspector? Surely it was day?" asked the Managing President.

"You are well informed, Mr. Poper, good. Yes, it was day."

"I was at a fundraiser, with my chaperone Miss Pierce and my chauffeur Yates. You can check with my files and that of other attendees of course."

"Of course, thank you. Now, Yates, yes," said Chapel, thinking a moment. "I was made aware he was a veteran of the Battle of Bal'tyx Grounds. You employed him after that?"

"Yes, he was a very messed up man," said Poper, simply. "I have seen the toll the Feuds have on many bright people and I am his sponsor. He runs me around and occasionally provides security."

"Very good. And you can account for him and another fellow, Mr. E'zello?"

"Ah, the good doctor E'zello," said Poper, smiling. "He is part of my chemical research team. I've been his student and now he works for me. A good man, with many accomplishments."

"He has a record on several planets," said Chapel, again simply.

Poper laughed. "Speeding and parking tickets. He is very forgetful and a bit of a racer in his spare time. Yes, he is accounted for. He is currently overseeing a shipment of equipment for his labs work."

Chapel nodded, seeming satisfied. "Very well, Mr. Poper." He turned to look at the two paintings on the walls.

"I see you have an Anton Fellis, admirer of his work?" Chapel cocked an eyebrow at the 3D artwork in the corner of the office.

"Ah yes, the 'Fire Stoker'." Turning as DuSalle and Chapel did to the large holo'artwork on the left, DuSalle, who had been taking in the details of this interview felt more than a little left out. "Fellis was a great admirer of Gavin Chandler. Very interesting, this piece was commissioned by Kurt Mully, Chandler's deputy, after his friend's own tragic demise."

The holographic was awash with a light and colour. Flames wreathed two shadowy figures. DuSalle found it was possible to interpret their stance in several ways, as they looked on the verge of embracing, though from another perspective they could be struggling with one another or even the taller of the shadows could be seen to be pushing the other to the ground or into the path of the flames. Within the flames were two ambiguous, almost faces watching the two figures within centre of the frame, but DuSalle could not decide on their attitude to the two shades, or even if they were to have an attitude at all.

"So, you say that Clove arrived with you, Mr. Poper?" said Chapel, breaking the moment.

"Magistrate Clove was very comfortable aboard my ship, Inspector." He motioned to the two chairs in front of him, as he stood and sat in the wing backed chair. "Please, won't you sit?"

DuSalle joined Chapel while Pierce stood beside her boss.

"What kind of materials did he have with him?"

"Ah, that I could not say." He turned to Pierce. "Miss Pierce will provide you with a ship's manifest, if you wish, though I thought that was included in the government bundle you would have received on beginning this case."

Chapel smiled cagily, annoyed. "Oh, The Security Corps is merely a protective group. Government deals go a little beyond our range, Mr. Poper."

"It seems to upset you, Inspector," said Mr. Poper, a strange look in his eye.

"When we are forced to, 'pull strings' it is a little difficult in the Security Corps," said Chapel, "but we get by."

"I see. Well, any help I can provide catching his killer then, Inspector." He threw out his arms in an open gesture, while Chapel's hands remained in his lap. "Clove was a handsome man, maybe a jealous man or even woman was gunning for him."

"Personal more than political, then, Mr. Poper?"

"Maybe, Detective," said Poper. "He was never talkative on the trip I am told. I did have occasion to speak with him directly, though only with his office."

"I see," said Chapel. "So you were never to notice anything untoward about his behaviour?"

"No." Poper turned again to Pierce. "How about you, Kathryn? You worked closer with him than I."

DuSalle noted the slight colouring of Kathryn Pierce's cheeks as she was addressed. "No, I did not, Sir." She focused on Poper. "He was charming and forthright, wanted the talks to go well, spoke of little else." A small smile lit her striking features. "He was obsessed with the ideals these two governments could come up with, very passionate about it all." Pierce's face blanched as if she had said too much.

Poper however looked unperturbed by this, though Chapel's blink and miss it smile made a brief appearance.

"That I'm glad of, Miss Pierce." Chapel inclined his head. "It seems we have enough information from you, Mr. Poper, though I would say to step up your security in light of this incident."

Poper stood as Chapel and DuSalle rose to their feet. "Thank you, gentlemen," he bowed. "I am greatly honoured by your investigation. I hope you will uncover the assassin swiftly."

Chapel and DuSalle bowed in response, Pierce also bowing low. "Thank you for answering my questions, Mr. Poper."

As DuSalle and Chapel were shown to the door by Pierce, Chapel stopped to look at the 'Fire Stoker' again.

"One last if I may, Mr. Poper," said Chapel. Poper, who was still seated nodded. "When you saw the 'Fire Stoker', what was it that made you buy it?"

"Interest, Inspector, only interest."

"Thank you very much," said the Inspector, bowing again. "Good day to you."

XIII

Night had descended thickly over Chandler City. The mile length and height of the domes in the Eastern Quadrants were beginning to fog up from the moisture rising from the genetic forests that ringed the outer edges of the Domes, creating a walled off citadel within each Quad. The breathy sucking tone of air filters ticking over mixing with the horrid inducing cooing and chattering of genetic creations filled the night air above the low vibrating murmur of traffic.

Hanging a mile and a half above the dense floor of the genetic forests, Wilbit Marcson clipped the synth-rope through the hook and threaded it through his gloved fingers to give him a bit more slack so that he was swayed in the gentle breeze, connected to the infinite lattice work of high density steel struts and seventy inch thick plastic coated glass that protected the colony city from the harsh toxic atmosphere of Pelimar.

Just seventy inches was between him and instant death, but Marcson was used to that, having previously worked on high iron structures of the Habs on Mars Point, much to the dismay of his well-to-do sister; though she was only well-to-do after marrying one of the Mining Barons of Proxima, who in the hopes of becoming a multi-trillionaire was eager to land a seat on the Inner Dynastical Congress. Even become a Dynasty name.

Marcson had other plans, however. He had been young when contact had been made with Pelimar and its single colonial city. He had set out from under the protective wing of his older sister who had cared for him after the death of their mother and father in a Ray burning disaster on Strothcor VII.

He carved himself a decent career as a Bio-Dome engineer. He loved working with the delicate structures. As sensor plates, vehicle detection and aversion systems were in constant need of maintenance, there was also now the unique 'weather' program that had been devised some six hundred years ago, in an effort to give the citizens a feel of a more habitable place rather than thinking about the venomous clouds that hung in the sky making the sun, Peli, shine a dull brown on occasion.

Marcson had marvelled at it, as it was able to create seventy levels of rain. With temperate manipulator variations over the city it was easy to adjust from a heavy mist all the way to snow fall, though it was a hell of a system when it needed to be de-bugged or virus protected.

He guided himself toward the slide pole to his left, where he would be able to exit down into the next grid of grips and cable holds that surrounded the lower bank of air compensators.

He had worked well into the evening, checking his silver plated chronometer every few decs. It had been present from his sister, when she had come into money. She had preened over it more than Marcson had, though of course he put on the show. He did not want to disappoint her, after all, even if his plastic one was in fine working order.

He had chosen this type of chronometer for its durability, as a hobby he was into judo and karate, not that he got far with it, but he knew the basics. He needed it with the gangs that roamed the streets of a night, and it was something he had only considered after he heard about them from his neighbours.

Marcson was due his dinner break now. In fact he was a few minutes over. He hurried down to the lower platform, finally lowering his feet to the welcoming ground. As he turned shrugging off the straps of his equipment, he heard the tell-tale clang of someone ascending the ladder from the lower platform.

He looked around as his replacement should have been there to meet him to take over duty for an hour.

"Hey, Mal, what kept…" he stopped as a neatly shaven head appeared over the lip of the platform instead of Malcolm Wyles' curly reds.

He stared dumbfounded as the refined looking features of this woman stared at him as though he was nothing, as if he was a speck of dirt on her booted feet which had to be removed.

"Can I help you, Officer?" he said, noting the uniform of a Security Corps Constable, under the heavy red pseudo leather jacket.

Her lip turned up in disgust and she stepped forward.

"You filth!" she exclaimed. "You dare come here and take away our lives!"

Marcson frowned at the strange woman, then reflexively dodged as she aimed a punch at his head. The gauntlet clad fist clipped his ear, sending him against the rail. He yelled, grabbing the rail, turning toward the Constable whose features were screwed up in hatred.

"What the…" he exclaimed, but again he had to dodge to the side as she aimed a kick to his ribs.

Marcson threw himself forward in a tackle move, his shoulder forward. His head bent down, he managed to grab her around her slim waist, aiming to throw her against the opposite rail. Her fist came down hard on his back as his hand was barely around her waist.

He felt it crack as the Constable's knee shot up into his stomach, throwing him to the side. Screaming in pain, sure that not only had he broken his collar bone but also his back, he rolled to the side with the woman's foot assisting him.

Then Marcson found himself rolling still, right over the rail and into the air. Some deep rooted survival instinct or karate movement enabled him to grab hold of the rail as he rolled over it.

He tumbled over, the pain roaring through his body. As his arm jerked and his back strained, Marcson's tear-stricken face looked up the Constable. She stood over him, not smiling nor laughing, just looking at him.

"Please!" he gasped.

"Do it, Constable, finish the scum," a voice said from behind the woman, who was glaring menacingly down at Marcson.

"Please, no!" he moaned as he reached up with his other hand to grip the rail.

"Now!" shouted the voice. Marcson felt all the pain in the world centre on the knuckles of his right hand as they were crushed by the weight of her gloved fist. His fingers, numbed and useless, let go of the rail before his other hand could reach.

He fell straight down – he did not tumble, did not hit anything on the way down. He landed in a boneless heap through an opening in the leafy canopy into the genetic jungle.

Life had not left Will Marcson yet.

He was quickly submerged in soft quicksand. Through his battered features he sighed with relief, throwing out an arm to catch hold of a thick root that was beside him and dragging himself free, finally saved.

Until his eyes set upon a large muscular and fanged creature, which was not human or alien in any form; it swooped forward, faster than he could blink.

Massive jaws snapped his head clean from his body, the outstretched arm still gripping the thick vine in the middle of hauling Will Marcson's body clear of the weak quicksand.

XIV

DuSalle scanned over his report for a third time, making the last of the corrections before he was sure to file it to the top secret folder.

He had finally finished after two hours, it was now closing in on midnight and small pinpricks of brownish moonlight filtered through the cloud layer of toxins to cast its glow over his sparse apartment.

So much had happened over so little time. DuSalle felt at once glad but highly strung out over the events. Only a certain amount of information had gone into his report.

Not his conversation with Chapel on his 'Method' or his comments to the landlady or the Security Corps' capabilities to police the city, or even Brig's aside about the Inspector's links to the IJ Section, either.

The Detective had learned long ago to keep certain things to himself, at the cost of a stint in the Interrogation chair in the Internal Judicial Section chambers, maybe, but they were trivial to the investigation as a whole.

It had been secrets that had bonded him to his schoolmates, even at their cost and his promotion. It should not have been him after all to become Detective. Then again, Yally was dead. He had been made an honorary Detective but at the cost of his life.

DuSalle still shuddered at thoughts that crept into his mind, but it was enclosed spaces that confounded his reason and his senses. In the Eastern Quads there was not much chance of that being a major problem for him. With domescrapers and high flying vehicles, it was likely he would not have his feet touch the ground of Street level, unlike if he were still in the Western Quads.

The Detective tiredly switched off his console and was about to turn in for the night when his flat buzzer went off.

Wearily, he traipsed over to the door and touched the contact.

The door slid open and standing there was not Inspector Chapel, as DuSalle had expected to call on him in the middle of the night.

It was, in fact, Councillor Unisa Balla.

Though this was not the Balla he had seen in Chief Vice's, the Councillor's demeanour seemed completely different.

"May I come in, Detective DuSalle?" asked the Councillor in a low, rather sultry tone.

"Of course, Councillor," DuSalle started, hating the squeak in his normally smooth voice. He moved aside to let the Councillor into his suddenly modest and rather emotionally barren flat. She was dressed in a techno-print faux-mink coat.

Balla stood in the middle of the room. Her sharp gaze seemed to be softer than he remembered as she took in the living area, though DuSalle had yet to fully settle in after only a few days.

"May I ask what brings you here, Councillor?" he asked. As she moved swiftly into the living area the Councillor perched herself on the low sofa furthest away from the Narrocaster display, but closer to the small thermal vent that DuSalle had switched to a higher setting.

"Straight to business, I like that," smiled Balla, openly. "Don't stand on ceremony, Detective. I hate to be craning my neck through this entire talk."

"Yes, of course." DuSalle chose the lone squashy chair that was turned away from the Narro-caster to face the Councillor, who had on small stiletto heeled boots.

"I know that you have only just finished your report," she said, her honey eyes locking with his, "but instead of just reading pixels on a screen, I would like your personal opinion on a few matters, DuSalle."

"Yes, er, well – what would you like to know?"

"Again, no chatter," Balla smiled again. "That is so refreshing." Balla moved along the sofa so that she was only a short distance away from DuSalle. She took off her long coat, revealing an alluring gold and brown tightly fitting outfit underneath. "Well, for one, what have you discovered, about Clove particularly? Was he as he seemed?"

"From the reports and the details we've read from the files you supplied, yes. He was a clone, but they were taken and developed from birth, so virtually he was a twin. The original cell donor was killed in an aircraft crash on Ly'tel Asteroid Belt fifteen years ago," said DuSalle, rattling off all the information he could recall. "But you know this, right, Councillor."

"Mmm." She nodded. "I wanted to know your take on the man."

"He was a womaniser as far as I could see." DuSalle frowned. "But that's his personality. As to his work, well, it seems he was genuine in that. From the files again the truce he was working on seemed to be something to think about."

"You understood it?" asked Balla, surprised.

"Well, no," admitted DuSalle. "It was a lot of statement-like language, but it seems the general idea was a sharing of information and technologies, even bringing in people from their side and ours to sort through ideas that may be workable together."

"Working together," mused Balla. She stared into space for a moment. "That is a dream indeed, to see the outside world, all it's ... treasures, that I'm sure are many."

"It's a work in progress, yes." DuSalle frowned as a niggling thought was brought to his attention, away from Balla's rather striking profile. "Forgive me, Councillor, but aren't you... well, in Kelly's party?"

"I am, DuSalle," she said, almost warily. "However, it seems I may not be for longer. That's one of the reasons I am covering this case." She stood up suddenly, walking to the other end of the room.

DuSalle also stood, a strange feeling rising in the pit of his stomach as he looked at the suddenly fragile figure in front of him.

"It may be time for a change. Kelly is not the man... that he once was, DuSalle... nor..."

"Yes, Councillor?"

"This is highly irregular," she said suddenly, looking over at the genetically stunted crawlers that were positioned at the four corners of the room, tendrils latched onto the walls, seeking out light and moisture unlike their more feral cousins in the Genetic Forests.

"It was not my idea," said DuSalle apologetically, though not knowing why he felt like this. He moved closer.

Balla turned a quizzical gaze on the uncomfortable Detective.

"The plants, I mean." He gestured to them and her expression suddenly relaxed into an amused stare.

"It was not the plants I was referring to, DuSalle." She smiled.

"Oh," was all that came out.

"I refer to coming here so late at night." She looked him up and down, still smiling. "I've often wondered how a Security Corps Officer lives. Is it true you completely abstain from... how shall I put it... companionship?"

"Yes – yes, that's ah correct, Councillor," at once feeling he was on shaky ground, while all was quiet, like the eye of hurricane. "It's been that way since the SC was founded by Mully and Benefactor Chandler. It was introduced to starve off corruption, something that Mully knew was rife in the ESU."

"The Enforcer Service Units? You mean the old Planetary Union police force?" said Balla, facing DuSalle and moving closer.

"That's correct, Councillor."

"Then you have… never ever known the touch of a woman?" she asked, closing the gap between them. "Why so nervous, DuSalle?"

"I'm not nervous," said Detective, shaken.

"Then why are you backing away?" The Councillor advanced again, sucking on her bottom lip. DuSalle's eyes were drawn to the movement.

Mentally he tried to kick himself into gear, to not be swayed.

DuSalle stopped backing off, but the Councillor kept advancing until they were barely a foot apart.

"Councillor Balla… I," said DuSalle, not in the stern voice he had wanted, but in a bare whisper. The Detective's body began to shake with long forgotten urges, boiling to the surface, as the Councillor continued to close the gap between them.

"Unisa, DuSalle," she whispered.

DuSalle must have looked confused, as Balla smiled seductively, chuckling. "My name, DuSalle, that's my name."

"Oh," said DuSalle, his body no longer tense. As she moved even closer, their faces were now mere inches apart.

It may have been the higher pitched hum, which was not coming from the thermal vent, or it may have been the split second that DuSalle's gaze shifted from her lips to her eyes which were no longer hooded with desire, but wide with alarm, that made him grab the Councillor and push them both to the floor.

As the thick armoured glass of his flat exploded inward, showering the Detective's back with splinters of armoured Ne'er-Brek glass.

XVI

"Salle, I do suggest you wake up now," said Inspector Chapel's voice, from somewhere far off to the Detective's left, "or you really will never be able to live this down in the Base locker rooms."

"Sir?" DuSalle opened his eyes, but had to instantly shut them again as the blinding light dazzled his numb mind for a moment. "Where…"

"I'm not sure, Detective, looks like a storage space in La Flayed Dragon," said Inspector Chapel from his left. DuSalle heard a shuffling of clothing from his right, meaning someone else was there. "I was about to ask the Councillor."

The previous hours in DuSalle's flat came back to him – the writing up of his report, the Councillor's appearance and the Councillor's…

DuSalle's eyes snapped open.

He immediately turned to the right in the brightly lit room to see Councillor Unisa Balla bound as he was. A bright intense light was coming from three small squat gravity generators on top of a stack of crates marked 'LFD – CONDIMENTS', which was holding them captive against the wall. Sensors were attached to their wrists, chest and ankles.

A gag was in Balla's mouth. DuSalle tried to communicate reassurance without words as he looked in to her large frightened eyes.

"Funny, Detective," said Chapel. "I was brought here first alone, but they brought you both here at the same time." He raised an eyebrow.

DuSalle stared at Chapel for a moment. "S-sir, I – I… it…"

"Detective," Chapel began, but on the far side of the small room the bulky storage door slid open and three men in leather armour and ebony sprayed facemasks stepped into the room.

The two stood either side of the first smaller one to enter. They were stockier and thick set than the first, both of which were holding sonic blasters.

"I wouldn't use those if I were you," said Chapel. "Firing those while the gravity field is active, shall we say, will cause quite a mess."

"Know why you're here?" said the thickset one on the leader's left.

"You're with the People's Island Movement, isolationists. You've been spying on us," said DuSalle, balling his fists, not wanting to look at Balla, as several thoughts congealed like hot soya beans in his stomach. "Wanted a more direct approach, right?"

Balla moaned through her gag as Chapel levelled a look at the three men.

"DuSalle, DuSalle, DuSalle," came a distorted but familiar voice from behind the blank mask of the lean figure. "I did say we would meet again, did I not?" He removed his mask, revealing a familiar face. "Though isn't it a shame it is not under better circumstances?" It was Second Official Julian Cartier and he was smiling warmly.

"Yes, you did," said DuSalle, trying to hide his surprise behind his sudden rush of contempt. "Why –"

"Why this?" asked Cartier, smile widening. "I'm sorry to say, your investigation was getting too close and being too harmful to our movement, DuSalle. I must uphold Balla's innocence, at least in this current matter." He glared at the

Councillor. "But from what I gather from your rather intimate conversation, she is not totally innocent." He turned back to DuSalle. "You, Detective, suspect our leader. I cannot allow you to take him in. I cannot allow you to besmirch his respectable name."

"Kelly is hardly respectable, Cartier," said Chapel. He looked amazingly calm for someone captured by a group that could easy kill him without thought. "A regular gambler, a womaniser. Also and more importantly, he is not the leader of your particular group. Kelly would not kidnap and brainwash an officer of the Security Corps, for example."

Cartier glared at Chapel. "How do you know about that?"

"The murders of Prenbrett Sullivan and Wilbit Marcson," said Chapel, heatedly. "Possibly others who came here in the last three months. Just how did you get those names, Cartier?"

"We did not assassinate anyone," said Cartier, turning to DuSalle, imploring. "Nor did Kelly. You must know this to be true, DuSalle."

"Why should we believe you, Cartier?" said DuSalle trying to think, trying to move, he looked over at Balla again, who was staring at Cartier but not really seeing him. She was staring through him, beyond him. "How can I believe you after you take all of us like this?"

"There is more than one Isolationist movement in Chandler City. We of the People's Island Movement," said Cartier, gesturing to his stocky colleagues, "have staged a few bombings, true." His smile widened again. "But what we are planning is much more than that we want to prove our point. These people are not welcome, it's not their city, what do they care about us, what we do?" The admin's face hardened grimly. "So far we have not been too overtly public about who we have retired, shall we say, but soon we will have a greater target, thanks to Councillor Balla's helpful files."

Balla moaned through her gag. DuSalle was trembling with rage, but Chapel seemed the most composed with his legs spread apart and arms above his head.

"La Flayed Dragon," he said, managing to turn his head and nod toward the gravity generators settled on the marked crates. "Make an example of us all, eh?"

"Exactly, Inspector, exactly right." Cartier grinned again.

"You don't know anything about the assassination, then," said DuSalle, "about what's being planned?"

Cartier shrugged. "As much as you know, only as much as this," he turned a disgusted look on Balla, "this traitor and whore knows, DuSalle." He motioned to one of his bodyguards. "Take that gag out, as she seems to be dying to add something to this little convention of ours."

Cartier's man on his left holstered his sonic weapon and approached Balla, pulling the cloth away from her mouth.

"That is all very useful to us. You'll be arrested in short order," said Balla, in a level voice, not betraying the fear that had shown in her darkened eyes.

"Interesting how Councillors gain more confidence when using their voices, isn't it DuSalle?" asked Cartier, glaring at Balla. "Take that away and they become helpless waifs."

"You're not getting away with this. Cartier, was it?" continued Balla. "Kelly will not be the only one displeased with this."

"Think Kelly cares, Balla?" spat Cartier. "You had him tied around your little finger far too long. He saw you for what you were, then you got into the deep end. It's time you all drowned in the lies you insist on perpetrating."

"You hate us for all the wrong reasons, Cartier," said Chapel with an icy calm. "Your hatred of me, unlike DuSalle and Balla here, is personal, very much an isolated anger."

"Don't joke..."

"Cartier, I cannot change what happened to your sister!" said Chapel as Cartier's face contorted with rage.

"You were the one that arrested her! You were the one that interrogated her!"

"And she left with her pride and dignity intact, Cartier. She left the Corps of her own free will! What happened to her after that was not of my doing!" Chapel said, over Cartier. "You cannot change the past, Cartier, as you cannot and will not change the future," he said forcefully. "I am not an IJ anymore, merely a Street and that I wish to remain. You however…"

"Enough!" shouted Cartier, drowning out Chapel. The guards on either side hefted their sonic weapons as DuSalle and Balla were also about to interject.

"You three will die for a worthy cause. This city will awaken to a new order," said Cartier. His features were calm, though his voice trembled with anger. "The Outsiders, the Stels and the Regs, will be cast out and they will no longer infect this fine city."

"If you truly believed that, Cartier, you would have set off the bombs by now," said Chapel. "You hesitate, Cartier. Now there are too many of these 'Outsiders' in our city. How are you to be rid of all of them?"

"You'll work it out eventually, Chapel," he spat, pulling his mask over his wrinkled features. "But by then it'll be too late for you and your Outsider friends, Bon voyage, Inspector."

"Resonator or a simple explosive?" asked Chapel, suddenly, as though asking about an item of clothing rather than the method of their deaths.

"Explosives, Chapel. It's the only way to make a poignant point."

As the three started to back out of the small storage space, the door slid open again, but there was someone behind them.

"Oh, sorry, ladies, did I interrupt a terrorist meet?" said a voice from behind them.

The terrorists turned quickly as one, raising their weapons to the intruder, but Cartier's man on the left snagged their sonic gun on the corner of one of a crate which knocked over the gravity generators out of alignment with the three captives.

Chapel was free first, as the isolationists took aim on the intruder, who had leapt to the side.

The Inspector charged at the closest isolationist, who was nearer the crates.

The isolationists fired their sonic weapons, just as the gravity generators were knocked off the crates, freeing both DuSalle and Balla, just as the intruder wildly returned fire, laser bolts missing the Detective and the Councillor and hitting the hard floor.

The wall surrounding the door broke apart as Chapel and the isolationist crashed to the floor themselves.

DuSalle scrambled to his feet and ran at the attacking isolationists.

Cartier turned just as DuSalle's foot smashed into his face, while his fist thudded into the other isolationist's kidneys, pushing them both into the corridor.

DuSalle landed on top of the first isolationist and punched him twice before he was unconscious, turning to Cartier who aimed a kick at his side.

Chapel knocked out the other isolationist as the intruder rose to her feet.

"Ah, good," said Chapel, punching Cartier, who had half risen to his feet. "Free at last."

Balla joined them in the corridor as Chapel pulled off Cartier's mask to look him straight in the eye.

"Arrest him, Inspector," said Balla, imperiously.

"Now, Cartier," said Chapel. Holding the now smiling Cartier, DuSalle frowned down at the man who had introduced him to the Eastern Quads. "You will tell us, all you know about Clove."

Cartier smiled, in Chapel's grip, his jaw working. "Never!" he shouted.

"Blast!" said Chapel, releasing the suddenly immobile terrorist. "Suicide pill, I'm afraid. A replaced tooth, I suspect."

DuSalle gulped, as he watched Cartier crumple to the ground, lifeless. "Now what do we do, Sir?" asked DuSalle, as Chapel helped him up, facing him and not looking down at Cartier's inert form. "We haven't anything to go on."

"I wouldn't say that, DuSalle," said Chapel, staring at Cartier's body also, but seeming to look beyond it. "The weapon and the document might be something to go on, though, as he said, he only knew what we knew about this." Chapel sighed.

"I hate to interrupt, but didn't he say something about a bomb?" exclaimed Balla.

"Yes, he did mention that, didn't he, Councillor?"

XVII

The team of constables Chapel had called in over his open-channel radio, had stormed the storerooms of *La Flayed Dragon* and arrested half the staff of the pilot's bar, whilst DuSalle, Chapel and Balla were all taken to the nearest Emergency centre.

The fusion bomb which Cartier's surviving men had given over the whereabouts to had been quickly found and then safety detonated, while Cartier and the bodies of his followers were taken away by the Forensic unit.

DuSalle and Balla were being treated for their cuts and bruises, caused during the attack on DuSalle's flat, when a relatively unscathed Chapel entered the examination room.

"Excuse me, Medic," he addressed the 'bot tending to Balla's back. DuSalle sat more to attention, wincing slightly as the 'bot attending him sealed another cut on his back and he was jolted by the movement. "But I need a word or two with the Councillor."

"I have nearly finished tending to the Councillor and the Det…"

"Now, if you don't mind," said Chapel, in a commanding tone.

Though DuSalle knew 'bots of this low grade work did not have an emo'chip, he could have sworn as the two 'bots left the room that they were decidedly put-out.

"Exactly what questioning requires that I am not to be fully treated, or fully clothed, Inspector?" asked Balla, in the same imperious tone she had used on Cartier, while holding a heavy bed sheet over her chest.

Like Cartier, Chapel was not amused or concerned by her attitude, nor by her half-nakedness.

"The moment you are 'fully treated', Councillor, you will be whisked away by the Benefactor's own guards, for 'debriefing'. But I, and I'm sure Detective DuSalle, here, have a few rather awkward questions before that happens, which need urgent resolution, the resolution to this very case, Councillor Balla."

Balla frowned as DuSalle gingerly pulled on his tunic and joined Chapel. Something in her demeanour seemed to collapse at that moment. "Continue then, Inspector," she said, dejectedly.

"Thank you, Councillor," said Chapel, smiling sharply. "We all know there was something going down with the Stels. They have been in a state of war for a long time, but their new line seems to be in diplomacy and treaty bargains. Odd, no?" The Inspector looked from DuSalle to Balla.

"You mean there is no truth to this treaty and they don't intend to honour it?" Balla frowned.

"I know nothing of politics, Councillor," shrugged Chapel. "I only know investigations, crimes of emotion and the mind, for instance your affair with Clove and Kelly and the Benefactor."

"I don't..." Balla looked scandalised, while DuSalle's mouth hung open in shock and surprise at the Inspector's rather simply put but highly scandalous statement.

"Ah," said Chapel, "it was rather easy to figure out. Clove was an appealing and very charismatic man, a bit of a womaniser also, I might add." Balla barely winced but DuSalle saw her shoulders drop. "But you were in the isolationist business. You have got involved in something over your head, Councillor."

"I will not..."

"No, you will," said Chapel, over her, heatedly. "You were first with Kelly, a strong and rebellious man, you were attracted to him straight away. Kelly was never able to settle down, but that also suited you, because you hate the stillness of life, correct? Then came chaos and rebellion, no one embodied its truer form more than Clove, right Councillor? You gravitated to him with a much easier relationship than Kelly, a fire and heat that was smouldering the day you met, 'til the day he met his end."

"That…"

"Is not all I have to say, Councillor. You fell for these men in the simplest of terms. While they saw a kindred spirit in you, they were attracted like moths to a flame. But that is what attracts you also, those who go against the order of things. But they were mere flings, compared to the Benefactor."

"What?" blurted DuSalle finally succumbing to his shock.

"Oh, yes, Detective," said Chapel, giving the Councillor a look of utmost distain. "Rocking the order of things to its core, right, Councillor? Attempting to change this planet forever. The man you wished to protect more than even yourself." Chapel focused on Balla, moving so close to her that all she could was to look at him. "Because you believed him responsible for Clove's death, didn't you?"

Balla's face which had been as steady as a rock suddenly crumpled in distress.

"Now, the Benefactor and everything that we exist for is in crisis. The fate of this city lies in your hands, Councillor. I wish to know how it all happened – how you got involved with Clove and who was behind his arrival here."

"What importance is that, Sir?" said DuSalle, caught between wanting to comfort the distraught looking Councillor and to not want it.

"Seems I may have been a tad too harsh about the point you made earlier, DuSalle." The Inspector was giving him an appraising look as he said it.

"The Docking Bays, you see, DuSalle. Clove has brought more than diplomacy to this city, though he may not have known it. Drugs, perhaps more."

"Impossible," said Balla, seeming to come out of the horror struck trance which Chapel had induced in her. Then she gasped with realisation, "You can't mean the ship he arrived on. It was checked and vetted."

"Untrue," said the Inspector as he stared hard at her. DuSalle tried to detect any deceit in her trembling voice. "Diplomatic shuttling and transport of both the Stellar Sovereignty and the Pastoral Regions have been exempt from such searches, vetoed by the Chamber of Patrons thirty years ago."

Balla gasped again. "No, that's not... couldn't be... I can't... won't."

"True, I'm sorry to say, Councillor." Chapel looked at DuSalle.

DuSalle straightened up gingerly. He put on a hand on the Councillor's now hunched shoulders. "We need the name of the contact that Benefactor used to ferry Clove here, the one that was not included in Poper's report – the one that could help us clear all of this up for good, Balla."

DuSalle looked her in the eye with the kindest expression he could muster. As the facts were slotting into place in his mind and trying hard not to show his contempt for this now broken woman, who could have possibly put the whole of the city on the front lines of an interstellar war. "Tell us, Councillor. It could be a disaster if you don't. Tell us the name of the contact."

Balla's lips trembled. DuSalle softened his expression, ignoring Chapel. "He was a very charming man, much like Clove... I can't ..." she said slowly, looking straight at

DuSalle, pleading for him to understand, but as he focused on her, Balla's honey eyes hardened to icy gold. "His name… And I promise I'll get you the all the data on him." Balla swallowed hard as she spoke again, her voice was as harsh as the toxic winds that swirled around the domes of Chandler City. "His name is Iverberg."

XVIII

The man who was only recently referred to himself as Aaron J. Hiven-Iverberg, sat bolt upright from his king sized anti-gravity four poster bed, his hand stalling the scream that had jumped up into his throat straight from his unconscious.

Iverberg, as he liked to be called, wiped a hand over his damp forehead, the nightmare visions already fading from his mind, as he tried to recall the illusive strands of thought that had brought them about.

The slim pale hand curled around his hip sent them reeling back into the darkness as he looked down at the red curls splashed across the air cushioned white satin. His dark features, one more attribute that until recently was not his, flexed into Iverberg's lady-killer smile.

Here he was, in plush apartments provided by the organisation that funded his high cost lifestyle, in bed with a woman that three months ago would probably have cut him in ways to make him a useless lump of flesh and was now curled up beside him after a rather wild night of passion.

Iverberg was not particularly surprised at this situation. He was known in the organisation as a womaniser. Though it was more specific to say he had bedded several species, whether male or female, somewhere in his family history he was sure his ancestors had mated with another species other than human – not actually rare in the Stellar Sovereignty.

He had honed his skills of manipulation for many years to a peak that none could deny his charms. Having only been here a short while, he had managed to snare several women into his trap.

Iverberg looked over the plush bedroom which was much roomier than his previous quarters aboard the *Silver Frame*.

Careful not wake the sleeping woman, he slipped out of bed and crossed to the walk-in wardrobe, another plus to his employer's pay-out. He dressed quickly into a pale tailored executive suit with an ornate collar pin and red silk handkerchief in the breast pocket. He fastened on his wrist-comm. and slipped his Flat-entrance key card into his right pocket of his loose trousers, pulling on his worn brown space boots, the only thing that remained of his original gear before he had joined with the organisation.

"Lookin' sharp," he whispered under his breath, at his mirror image, flashing his lady–killer smile again.

He smoothed a hand over his shaven head, along the elaborate dragon tattoo that ran from his left temple to under his collar bone.

He left without hurry, grinning as he past the toppled bottle of champagne and the knocked over champagne flutes on the expensive faux-animal skin rug in front of the still fiercely burning holo' fireplace.

Iverberg turned to the storage cupboard in the ornate hallway where one important item lay in wait for him.

He had brought with him three cases, two suitcases carrying most of his life, carrying with several more stylish, fashionable and tailored attire, along with various pieces of expensive but fake jewelled pieces.

His third case however, was not a suitcase, in the way it was not for any use as luggage. Iverberg picked up the case and left the flat.

He travelled down several stories in a descend shaft, then several more up in a ascend shaft, crossing over a connecting walkway between the close Stakk-Flats.

He slipped into a public cubicle and changed into a darker version of his suit, before waiting ten minutes. He exited quickly and took another descend shaft. Iverberg then entered an internet café, having booked a private soundproofed booth.

He made his breakfast order at the bar, taking it over to terminal and settling in.

Iverberg thumped the slim attaché case on the desk top and opening it up, he pulled out a small round object and set it down by his side. The diode on the top flashed on and off for several seconds then stayed on.

"Bubble on," murmured Iverberg, grinning.

Then he pulled out the main piece of equipment which he had brought with him across the galaxy. The pieces by themselves were unspectacular to even the most thoughtful eyes that could and, given his grievous backstabbing reputation and his circumstances, would look over them while he was not there.

He set a holo-plate over the small nuclear cell generator, hooking up the dial and decryption console to the holo-plate, then wiring it to the main terminal, before tapping in the code. He again checked his wrist chrono'.

Iverberg had two hours before his bodyguard's return to consciousness. He smiled to himself again as he typed in the decrypt code.

As the terminal glowed into life, so did the holo–plate.

The signal was being bounced around the city and into space for several milliseconds. On the third ring, as usual, a face appeared three inches above the glowing plate, half the size of a normal head.

It was wearing a frown.

"Yes, what do you want, Iverberg?" the head of the Narcotics Unit asked sternly.

"Hey, don't get surly with me, Officer!" Iverberg said with feigned bemusement.

"Get on with it," said the Unit Leader, tired of this routine. "What information have you got for me?"

"Tomorrow," said Iverberg, "the unloading will finish tomorrow night."

"Right," she said, her head dipping slightly out of view as she noted this info down. "Where?"

"Docking bay forty-six," said Iverberg. "Expect about ten guards," he lied, with a grin.

"Then I'll expect twenty guards," growled the Unit Leader. "Really think I'm stupid enough to trust everything you say?"

"When is the money going into my account?" asked Iverberg, a bit more seriously.

"Tomorrow evening, that…"

"No, no good. Make it a week tomorrow," said Iverberg. "They don't trust me, if they find that money I'm dead and you're in trouble."

"Who will find it?" asked the Leader, so casually. Almost too casually that Iverberg found himself answering.

"Oh, no," said Iverberg, tutting, "you don't get it that easy. When we meet then I'll give you the names, not now."

"Iverberg, you…" He cut the connection.

Iverberg looked at his watch again. He packed the equipment away into his case and then he then decided to eat his meal.

He returned to his flat, redressing back into his pale suit. He was walking down the corridor toward his door when he saw out of the corner of his eye a young woman with a shaven head dressed in a rather tightly fitting grey one-suit, looking at him with a strange blank expression.

Iverberg turned on his best lady-killer smirk.

XIX

DuSalle and Chapel later filed their reports by the early evening to Chief Vice, who was more subdued than the Detective had seen him. This was possibly due to the content of the reports he was given, though he gave little indication of that.

The Detective and the Inspector rode a descend shaft to the lower levels of the Quad Base.

As they travelled in silence, DuSalle thought over the last twenty-six and a quarter hours.

He had been through a lot, with several rather unique insights into city life in the metropolis, but mostly it had been a breathtaking experience. All his thoughts on the glory and the horrors of what he had previously been through did not seem to match up to what they were heading toward.

They only had a few days left, if Balla's word was still to be taken literally, shaky though that now seemed.

Councillor Balla was a strange one. DuSalle could not figure it out. She seemed such a tightly wound and strict person to begin with, then to be shattered, as everything she had built up around her was destroyed, all because of her feelings for another person.

Emotions were a destructive force. No wonder the Security Corps had forbidden such grand acts of emotions. It would only be the anarchy of the early years of Independence.

It was the shiny surface of the descend shaft that tipped off DuSalle to movement behind him. His reaction was pure instinct.

He pulled his *PummelFist* and aimed at the movement, only to find a *PummelFist* pointed at his face in turn.

"Sir?" he whispered, his eyes widening in shock, as Chapel looked at him coldly.

"I need to know something, Detective," he said, in a stern yet quiet voice, the same voice he had used while addressing Balla. "I need to know why – for what reasons you were sent here?"

"I was ordered to, Sir," said DuSalle, simply.

"It's never that simple, Detective," replied the Inspector. "I have been without a partner for past eight months, then here you are. I find it all awfully convenient."

"You suspect me, Sir?" said DuSalle, watching Chapel. His thumb was resting on the hair-trigger, the small nozzle glinting menacingly at DuSalle.

"Of course I do," he said, his grey eyes boring and probing into DuSalle's features, trying to discern some measure of guilt from him. "I'd even suspected Brig and Wane, idiots though they are. It's just you seem to be in the thick of this. I don't like that. I have a duty to protect this city and I will carry it out. The methods that I possess. I have allowed you to be privy, to an extent that I was comfortable with. No longer, Detective. What is your connection with Balla? What has she told you? What have you told her?" he spat the last part out.

"I'm doing my duty too, Sir," said DuSalle, turning to fully face the Inspector. "I have been straight with you from the beginning. I am your partner. Though that means little to you, doesn't it, Sir?"

"I speak of trust over duty, Detective," said Chapel. "That is a greater matter. How do I know you are not just spying on me and reporting back to Chief Vice or Balla, even?"

DuSalle stared levelly at Chapel for a moment. "I am not, Sir."

The Detective was surprised by the Inspector's next action. He holstered his own *PummelFist*, Chapel looking at him as though he had never seen him before, a look he had not even given him in *La Flayed Dragon*.

"Forgive me, DuSalle," he said, his voice level and calm again. "It is a first to trust someone else. I judged you wrongly from the start. I am guilty of the thing I resented in others. You are unique DuSalle, I must say."

"Sir?"

Chapel smirked. "Too green for your own good." He held up a hand to stop DuSalle's protest. "I merely mean that you have a questioning mind, a mind that is in motion, DuSalle, which is something I need, as motion requires a destination. This destination is the truth, is it not, DuSalle?"

"Yes Sir, it is."

"Then I'm going to let you in on what this is about – not just what we are dealing with at the moment. There is something much larger at work. These criminal cases that I have been… hah, languishing on, have all had a connected function. I have seen it as my own purpose to seek out this fraternity of criminals. They are not just deeply rooted in this city, DuSalle, but within the entire galaxy itself. And it all leads back to Cobble Industries."

"You have proof of that, Sir?"

A crestfallen look passed over Chapel's features, but was altered by a relaxed smirk. "None so far, DuSalle. Merely various heightened suspicions which my old Instructor would laugh me out of court with. But this Iverberg is a lead," said Chapel. "I'm sure of it."

XX

DuSalle didn't question the Inspector taking the wheel of his own battered patrol car. They flowed with the traffic. Chapel was quiet and intent, while DuSalle reviewed the pieces of evidence. Chapel had set up a separate comp–server to the one Councillor Balla had access to, as both Detective and Inspector felt that her judgement was suspect, but her being active was necessary for them to achieve their goal. Arresting a Councillor would cause an uproar within the Chamber of Patrons and a full government inquiry.

DuSalle noted that Chapel had pulled off the main sky-paths where they were given open spaces between the colossal buildings, into the low-cost and more swarming residence area of Chandler City.

"Just want to make a quick stop, DuSalle," said Chapel, as he lowered the patrol car to grubby looking platform. "See an old friend."

A small group of children, probably no more than eight or nine years old, were passing in an overhang at the back, while their parents or possibly older siblings were sprawled on the moulding greenery, catching the last of the filtered sunlight. To the left a heavy safety door to the interior was ajar.

DuSalle frowned at this, as they were in hot water already with Vice, but decided to go along with it. "Sir."

He followed the Inspector a pace behind, checking all around him. He didn't like the closed off feel of the platform. It made the hair on his neck stand up.

They entered the corridor and Chapel seemed to be checking off room numbers on his hands as he went. They passed through another partly open door, then Chapel stopped and turned and went to the door they had just passed.

"Here we go, Detective." He smiled at DuSalle and pressed the buzzer under the palm lock.

There was a rumble from inside.

"Yeah, what yer wantin'?" said a man's tried voice over the intercom.

"This is four-zero-three-six-two-dash-eight, yes? Lemuel Naming?"

"Yer, that's me!" exclaimed the voice, a little bored. "What?"

"Nebula are better viewed from the west point," said Chapel.

DuSalle looked at Chapel, comprehending, as Naming gave a shout.

"Quickly!" ordered Chapel, as he pressed his hand to palm lock. As he shouted his name, rank and override to the computer, the door slid open and DuSalle held up his *PummelFist*.

They were greeted by an unusual sight. Naming was down on the floor, with only a bed sheet around his slim waist, his livid white skin scrawled with tattoos, while his head was turned to the side. DuSalle could see he was breathing.

Crouched low over him his attacker, nothing covering her slim though compact and muscular dark form, smiled widely under a stream of long blonde dreads. She was holding a stun-truncheon.

"But they are brighter from the north," she said, in reply to Chapel. "Hi, Inspector, what brings you to this neck of the woods?"

"I would discuss that, when you have clothes on, Shortland," said Chapel, dryly. "You're disturbing Detective DuSalle here."

Shortland grinned widely. "Sorry." She turned and sauntered off down the corridor. "Make yourself at home, sorry about the mess. He'll wake up in an hour."

She turned a corner. "Living room is third on the left."

"Thank you, Shortland," called the Inspector, taking her directions. "Come along, DuSalle. Don't want to look like you were gawping."

"Yes, Sir," said DuSalle, shaking himself.

A while later, with Lemuel Naming handcuffed in the bedroom, DuSalle, Chapel and Shortland were in the small living room-cum-kitchenette, it was almost as grubby as outside. There were two badly scratched and broken leather chairs DuSalle found hard to sit on, while Chapel was absently pulling at a long thread. Shortland dressed in a denim one piece under neon yellow shorts and a small worn jacket and sat on a fading settee, which was leaning to one side. She was smiling at DuSalle which made him uncomfortable.

"So, Lemuel Naming," said Shortland. "How did you know, Sir?"

Chapel shrugged. "A basic leap of logic, Shortland. I simply needed to request something from you."

"By bringing me out of cover?" She cocked an eyebrow at Chapel, who seemed unbothered.

"Your friend is supervising Cobble Industries' latest delivery," continued the Inspector. "I needed an in point. I want to get a closer look at what they are delivering and I heard Narc wants in on it also."

"How could you have known where?" asked Shortland, sitting up, then she hunched down suddenly. "Damnit, Eagles came to see me!"

"Yes, I went to see her," he turned to DuSalle, "on a feeling. Didn't mean to leave you out, DuSalle." He turned back to Shortland. "She wouldn't say where she had you posted, though I saw the pale mud on her boots; the scratch on her left hand was from a quick getaway, she said." He looked at DuSalle. "Street gangs are little more prolific here. I made the connection." He shrugged. DuSalle closed his mouth with a snap.

"So what do you want me for?" said Shortland. "I'm undercover. I've been working at the docks for three weeks with no suspicious activity, though Eagles' convinced of something. Then I was ordered to get closer to a supervisor – so far zip! Now what is it you want?"

"Two things," said Chapel. "I want to have a closer look as I said. I also want in on the joint drugs bust you and Eagles are pulling off at Docking Bay forty-six."

Shortland turned to DuSalle. "Y'know, even after all this time, I always feel like a trainee, yeah?"

DuSalle felt the only response he could give would be too many words, so instead he flashed a sympathetic smile. "Yeah," replied Shortland, smirking. "Feelin' very green indeed."

XXI

With a call to dispatch to pick up Naming, Shortland joined DuSalle and Chapel.

They exited the shabby flat only to find six of the adolescent parents were no longer lounging in the setting sun. Their children gone, they were sat or standing around Chapel's patrol car, holding an assortment of weapons.

The silence of the courtyard didn't last long.

"Get the stinking Secs!" cried a mohawk-haired teen.

Four charged them, clubs raised. "Down! Pacify only!" shouted Chapel, letting the first swing of a bat land on his upraised arm from the leader, DuSalle and Shortland lifting their *PummelFist*s and raking cover fire by the feet of the other approaching youths.

"This is the Corps!" shouted Chapel, as his *PummelFist* connected with the jaw of his leather clad attacker. "You are under arrest! Cease and desist!"

"I don't think it's working, Inspector!" said Shortland, jabbing a youth in the stomach with her stun truncheon, then punching another in the face.

"We need cover, Sir!" said DuSalle, as two blue-haired youths with barbed chains jumped at him from the roof of the patrol car.

"Exactly where can we run for cover, Detective?" said Chapel, as two youths with sticks replaced their fallen friend.

DuSalle caught one of the chains on his truncheon, yanking the youth off his feet, still fending off the other with a swift kick.

They were surrounded and outnumbered.

Suddenly the plaza was ablaze of light. A voice boomed over the fighting officers.

"This is the Corps! Cease and Desist! You are all under arrest!"

In short order, as constable's descended from the floating wagon, the youths were subdued and taken away.

"I don't get it, Sir," said DuSalle later as Chapel, himself and Shortland were in his patrol car. "How can you think that it was Poper?"

"You're leaving me more in the dark here, Sir," said Shortland. "I dunno how I'm going to convince Eagles of this."

"Simple, DuSalle," said Chapel, patiently. "Poper is the nexus of this assassination, I know it. The Nul'ern system is infested with pirates, thieves and conmen. I will not rest until I have him and his volunteer of villains in jail."

"But how do you know he's guilty? Do we have proof?"

"Are you gonna include me in this or what?"

"Shortland," said Chapel, stiffly, "you have been taken off undercover. You will address me properly."

Shortland huffed. "Not officially, Sir."

"Better," muttered Chapel, "I think."

XXII

Narcotics Unit Commander Arlynna Eagles was not happy to have three new officers added to her small tactical team, but the signed order from a disgruntled Quad Chief Vice was enough to quieten any misgiving.

"You screw up, you better not blow our team too, get me, Inspector?" the tall scarred Eagles had exclaimed, looking up from Vice's plastic sheet.

It was a rush job. Eagles had barely gone over the finer points of the operation and time was tight. It was now dusk as they crossed the swarming skies of Chandler City. They were following in the wake of the dark form of a redressed armoured transport, that was currently holding twelve Constables, two Sergeants and Chief Eagles.

They had been briefed prior to travelling to the Docking Bays, where they were to join the group as a whole.

Now DuSalle, Chapel and Shortland were travelling at a distance to the unmarked truck that was carrying Eagles and her unit.

Unlike the fully armed and fully uniformed squad, DuSalle, Chapel and Shortland were dressed in civilian clothing. Though Chapel retained his large coat and boots, DuSalle was in a basic brown faux-leather jacket and tunic, hiding his stab vest underneath, while Shortland had chosen a rather revealing top, short denim jacket and shorts, with large thigh-high boots.

"It's not like I can go up to the front gate and knock out the night duty guard, by asking the time, Sir."

"So long as you're polite about it, DuSalle," said Chapel.

The radio chirped. DuSalle picked up the handset. "This is pat seven-niner-four receiving."

"Call from forensics for Inspector Chapel."

"Accepted," said Chapel, loudly.

There was a click, then a familiarly dour voice spoke.

"Inspector," said Medic Flo'wynn, "I have made a discovery. Remember Clove's dragon tattoo?"

"Yes, go on, Flo'wynn."

"I had a few scans done. Turns out the tattoo was hiding microscopic capsules, containing…"

"Let me guess, Horizon?" said Shortland.

"Yes, that's correct. Who was that?"

"How much exactly?" said Chapel.

"Less than a 2 milligram dose, but enough to replicate," said the forensic. "Take about a month to replicate five full doses, probably longer."

"Thank you, Flo'wynn," said Chapel, over him. "Send your report to Vice, no-one else."

"Will do, Inspector. Flo'wynn out!"

DuSalle replaced the handset.

"So this Horizon, what is really, Sir?" said DuSalle.

"Dunno the med stuff, but it's basically it's a performance drug," answered Shortland, "like a cross between steroids and speed. This stuff has been on the market since some loon decided to plant sunflower seeds directly into the Pelimarian soil, the reaction of which caused a new hybrid species. It only went onto the market recently, making hauls double of the common drugs these days, better than the imported Stren or Hypo. Little over fifty people have died of overdose, but they were marked as unrelated by the Directorate, so not strictly illegal, unless in large doses." Shortland scowled.

"Horizon is a particularly nasty drug," she continued. "The pushers however peddle it on its single good point…"

"Strength and agility," cut in Chapel.

"Something any criminal around here would want to get their hands on." A slight sneer came to Shortland's heart-shaped features. "The majority of the after-effects are the usual drug taking affects – dependency on the drug and so forth. This drug is far more insidious than that though. It works through the immune and nervous systems, and the first basic muscle of a being, an adrenalin rush injected straight into the heart. The user, maybe after three or four times, will be a complete wreck, physically and mentally."

"Yes, *Helianthus-Noctus-Pelia*, I believe it's called," said Chapel, not turning around. "Sold well amongst the shipping traders, then to the person on the street. It spread like a brush fire."

"Right," said Shortland. "This stuff get you so hooked so hard you can do nothing else. In less than a week your body mass expands and you're able to do things beyond your first capabilities. Only seen a few of them, really strong, really quick. One woman was taking it, threw her wife through a plate glass window forty storeys up. She couldn't believe her own strength at the time. But then if you take away the drug, you go nuts. 'Get the Green-eye' as they call it."

"Green-eye?"

"Some weird reaction in the blood. It turns the pupil and iris green if they don't get a proper fix of it after a certain amount of time. Not sure how long, but still real freaky," said Staves, shuddering. "You can smell an addict a mile away too – burnt caramel, they reek of it."

"Can't they be weaned off it?"

"It's been tried. They just end up more weak. Their body functions just shut down. They become so committed to the stuff. It's like it just takes over the normal organ functions or something. Without an increased amount they just die. Sickened to the soul by it, but needing it like air."

"Horizon is not to ascend, DuSalle, but toward descent," said Chapel.

XXIII

"I've never been to the docklands before, Sir. How do they export from the Stel ships that come in?"

"The docking bays are placed underground," said Shortland, as Chapel's patrol car shot through tunnel after tunnel, "since the city lies on the edge of a cliff face. The only other way would be to build another set of domes, but you know how the Benefactor is about 'spending unwisely'."

"So it's all underground?" said DuSalle, with images of collapsing walls and roofs caving in whirling darkly through his mind.

Chapel must have heard the strain in his voice. "Don't worry yourself, Detective," the Inspector smiled. "These docking bays are older than the city – that's how the colonists built it. Upward," said Chapel, cheerfully. He slipped the patrol car under twin lanes of air traffic, descending to street-level.

The dome-scrapers slid away into the smaller and drably organised structures of trader shops, ship builders and repairers, then into the more bawdily elaborately decorated rest stops and cantinas.

Finally as they reached the slopping edge of the last dome, they reached street level, amongst the small out buildings and littered streets, which led into the Docking Bays. There were set against the imposing six hundred foot wall, setting the city apart from the roving genetic jungle.

They parked three blocks away from the Docking Bays Eagles' unmarked van also parked a discreet distance away. Though their entry was known to the Dock Master, this territory was owned by Cobble Industries.

DuSalle, Chapel and Shortland met up with Eagles and her group. She split them into two groups.

While Eagles' group would take the lower levels, Chapel's would take the upper. DuSalle was put into Eagles' group and Shortland was in Chapel's. With a brief nod to both Chapel and Shortland, DuSalle joined Eagle's group as one of her Sergeants cut through the chained fence at the back of the large property, leading through to an underground car park.

"Utah, cut through," whispered Eagles. "Everyone activate the signal jammers on their belts when I give the word." She handed her spare to DuSalle. "Keep this on you, radio silence 'til I say or we meet up with Chapel and Waris." DuSalle nodded, as Utah cut through the fence and the five Narc officers clambered through.

Flood lights set on the fence stayed dormant. As they crouched low and moved toward the florescent gaping mouth of the underground car park no guard was in attendance, so they walked past the closed gate and into the flickering light.

All had their *PummelFist*s drawn, faces tense for any movement.

There were very few cars in the lot. DuSalle was about to mention this when the lights suddenly clicked out.

"Night-vision!" came Eagles' harsh whisper.

They headed for cover by the cars. DuSalle looked about. Everything was green and dark, the other officers and cars blobs light and colour, then further in, a shape moved toward Utah.

Utah yelled and was lifted into the air. There was a loud crack. Utah was bent at a strange angle by the shape. DuSalle ducked as the screaming officer was thrown bodily against the bonnet of a '52 *Eclipse Stroller*.

The Narcotics Unit members scattered.

XXIV

Night had fallen on another day. Councillor Unisa Balla felt the rush of the coming day beyond tonight.

The day that would bring the Stellar Sovereignty to the doorstep of Chandler City, sat between the mighty empire and the rascal Pastoral Regions.

She however was packing her things. The Benefactor's guard had taken her to his office. She had attempted to explain but he would not hear any of it, only taking what he had read in the various reports. It had hurt and shamed her that her word no longer penetrated his hearing as it had done in the past.

Balla was angrier than she had ever been in her life – as if this was what she got for following her heart. It only led her deeper into destruction. She knew that now.

Time for a new start, a new life and a different place.

She was almost packed now, taking only her clothes and a few personal items. She would be rid of this place for good.

Her doorbell chimed but she ignored it, thinking back on the times with Clove, Iverberg and The Benefactor – the one she truly loved and the only one who had rejected her.

Maybe Iverberg would take her somewhere if she could sway him to take her on his ship.

That thought crumbled instantly in her mind. Chapel had been right. They had used her, used her diplomatic status and her body, her soul, to cripple this city under the weight of the Stel legions.

Cartier was right too. The chains of her shame and her neglected responsibilities weighed her down.

The door chimed again.

Hurriedly she stuffed her clothes into the last bag, wiping her tear-stained face and dragging her fingers through her hair. It spilled over her shoulders in dark waves. She set her shoulders, thinking of herself away from here, out of the umbrella of influence and free to do what she wanted.

Yes, she would go to Iverberg, to tell him what she thought of him, then she could leave and escape to another place – maybe within Stel space, maybe not – she didn't care.

The door collapsed inward from the massive weight of Security Corps footwear.

"This is the Security Corps! You are under arrest!"

Balla tore into the living room, incensed.

A young woman barely out of her teens, with a shaved head bared her teeth at Balla.

"What in the hell are you doing?" the Councillor yelled. "You have no right!"

Then she saw two shadowy figures behind her.

She glared at them. "So, it's as the Inspector said." She looked on the snarling youth. "This is your victim then, a young Constable?"

"She is no victim, Balla," spat the first. "She is a tool, once held by a traitorous outside and now controlled by us."

"I see. And what are you doing here, with your tool?" she spat back.

"We're doing what the Benefactor cannot and will not do," said the second figure, stepping behind the Constable and lowering his mouth to her ear, his lips moved, but Balla could not hear him. He looked coldly up at the Councillor. "We're cleaning up the mess."

When the Constable handed the figure her *PummelFist*, comprehension stilled Balla's movements. It was enough of a pause, as the figures entered with the Constable, replacing the door.

Balla turned to run but the Constable was on her, breathing harshly. She slammed her to the floor.

"You will pay, outsider!" growled the Constable.

"I am not an outsider!" called Balla, breathlessly. "I am one of you!"

"No," said the first figure.

"Do it, Constable!" urged the second.

The Constable punched Balla in the back. The Councillor gritted her teeth in pain, but didn't scream, she would not submit any more. She got a backward grip on the Constable's belt, then with a heave from her left foot planted on the floor, the Constable was flipped over Balla and onto her back.

Balla went to rise to her feet. The Constable's booted foot caught her in the face, tearing her lip. She stumbled backward into a glass cabinet.

The Constable rose to her feet, her grim features blank as a sheet.

"I am you, Constable," said Balla, looking the Constable in the vacant eye. "We have shared a man, who has shamed us both."

"Do your duty, Constable!" shouted the first figure.

"I can help you, Constable." Balla was not prepared for the tougher Constable. She rushed forward, throwing the Councillor into the glass cabinet. She stumbled blindly into the Narro-caster, the Constable slamming into her again.

The Narro-caster blazed on, showing an advert for Stel space.

"...come to another addition, Travel fans!" yelled the overly tanned Nedley Mewter, grinning pompously. "Why not travel away from it all with Adventure Tours...!"

Balla attempted to kick backward, but her foot was caught and she was thrown onto the floor.

She slammed her head into the cast iron coffee table.

"...travel to Telos, home of the floating penthouses, experience the wonder of the aerial views of the gas giant...!"

The Constable was on top of her then, slamming a fist into her face. Balla felt her jaw rage with pain, but did not scream. She attempted to grab the Constable, but the Constable's gloved hands were already on her throat.

"We – are the same!" choked Balla, as the Narro-caster nattered on. Holographic images of various locations and their planets winked by, with the cheery announcer grimly grimacing away.

"No," bit out the Constable, now straddling the Councillor, "we are not! I am Constable Chloe Warren and I serve the People's Island! You are filth!"

The world was shrinking down for the Councillor, as she clung onto life, she did not want to submit, but it all looked lost.

The two shadows appeared over the Constable's shoulder.

"Good bye, Councillor," said the first.

"Good travels, Balla," said the second.

Balla gritted her teeth, her airway was getting tighter. She grabbed the Constable around the throat with one hand. The two figures barked with harsh laughter while her other hand blindly seized a large shard of broken glass.

Her vision was fading now.

"Won't... submit... to... anyone!" she choked out and with a heave she slashed the Constable across the face.

The grip didn't falter, but as Balla's vision went dark, she was pleased that the laughter halted with horror. Hot droplets of blood fell into her mouth.

"...Good travels everyone, hope to see you out there!" said Nedley Mewter.

In her dying breath she tasted her victory.

XXV

Other shouts rang out and orders were barked into the echoing darkness of the carpool. DuSalle tripped and fell on his back to the tarmac. He crouched beside the bonnet of a '52 *Eclipse Stroller*. DuSalle scanned the area. Silence followed the brief chaos of a few seconds ago.

Except for a heavy breathing.

DuSalle looked up, bringing up his weapon. He saw a bright bulky shape standing over him. It grabbed him and pulled him upward, straight off the ground. Through the goggles that picked up the minimal light and maximised it, the figure's eyes glowed in the dark.

"What you doing here, soldier boy?" grunted the great hulking figure, gripping DuSalle's arm, forcing the weapon to drop out of suddenly limp fingers as the bones were crushed together. "Not going to be causin' trouble here, are ya?"

"Only for you!" said Chief Eagles from behind the figure. She fired twice, blinding DuSalle monetarily. He was dropped and with a guttural scream of rage the shape turned towards Eagles' position.

DuSalle scrabbled around for his weapon; he grabbed it and jumped to his feet. Eagles fired two more shots at the figure. DuSalle saw the silhouette of the great hulky creature walk calmly toward Eagles.

DuSalle fired off a shot at the figure, but the figure did not take any notice. Eagles screamed in pain. He let off another four fiery bolts at this creature, but Eagles' scream turned to rage and was cut off.

"Your woman is dead, soldier boy," said the figure, which was near invisible to DuSalle. "Now, it's your turn."

DuSalle waved the gun around hopelessly, to just fire off a random shot would be fatal, letting the monster know where he was.

Suddenly a large hand was around his throat. A breath of stinking hot caramel was by his ear, knocking off his goggles. "I'll be kind to you, soldier boy, as you've been a good sport," said the creature. Slowly DuSalle, slipped his *PummelFist* to his left hand, and reversed it. "I'll give you a quick death. I promise you won't feel anything."

"Thanks," choked DuSalle. He jabbed his right elbow into the creature's chest. "But I don't do things quick."

DuSalle dropped and turned in mid-air, firing six times at the creature before it finally dropped to the ground.

Standing, DuSalle holstered his weapon, and, taking a palm beacon out of his belt, found the light switch.

He found Eagles half stripped of her uniform, her intestines pulled out through her back, a terrible look of disbelief on her haughty features.

DuSalle turned his head away from the horrific sight. He headed for the door that led to the office and further up to the docking bay.

With weapon in hand he went up the metal staircase as fast as he could, while trying not to make a sound. He let out a breath he hadn't known he'd been holding, then he reached out a hand to open the door.

It exploded in his face.

XXVI

"...send someone quickly, I've got a Corps Officer here!"

DuSalle's senses came back to him one by one. He knew that he was now in the office. Keeping his eyes closed, he could hear the gentle hum of a computer and a soft murmur of a ventilator fan. His wrists were linked together by a pair of his own handcuffs, while his ankles were bound by rope. At least he assumed they were his handcuffs. He was lying on his back on a leather sofa.

"What do you meant you've got more important things to…" there was a pause, as the nervous voice changed. "Oh, I see you're awake. I know when my patient is faking it, you're not a very good actor, you know."

DuSalle gave up and opened his eyes to see that he was in the office after all. Above that was the docking bay. He looked directly at the man who had spoken to him.

He was short, dressed in a grey lab coat and tweed waistcoat, with a completely bald head with lined and sinister features on a square jawed seamed face, making him look like he had swallowed a sour lemon by accident. Over his left eye was a box, a red orb within staring bulbously at DuSalle.

Poper's Doctor E'zello.

"I may not be an actor, but I am an officer of the Corps," said DuSalle, levelly. "There are others on the way…"

"And they're going to rescue you, are they?" grinned his captor, heaving a long barrelled weapon onto his thin legs, as he sat to the side of the desk, he aimed it at DuSalle's face.

"With the amount of security we have here, you won't live long enough to tell anyone about it."

"About what?" he asked, flexing his fingers, his right gloved hand, hidden from E'zello, reached for the wrist of the left.

The old doctor grinned toothily again. "I'm not going to tell you. After all, you may escape. How would I live with myself then, eh?"

DuSalle smiled thinly back at him. "Who said you had to live through my escape?"

The man stopped grinning and with some difficulty lifted the weapon to again point at the Detective's face.

DuSalle moved quickly. Sitting up, having freed one hand, he punched his captor in the jaw, which sent the doctor against the desk, losing his grip on the weapon.

DuSalle grabbed his own weapon which lay on the table and pointed it at his former captor.

"I'm sure that weapon can do some damage," DuSalle smiled, "but this weapon can do damage too, especially at close range." He eyed the older man. "Personally, I don't think that you really want to die do you?" He lifted an eyebrow.

E'zello dropped the weapon with a grunt and DuSalle shot him with a stun bolt. The doctor fell to the ground limp.

Untying his legs, DuSalle picked up the long barrelled weapon while he holstered his gun. After tying up his former captor, he went over to a small spiral staircase that went up into the docking bay.

Things were a little too quiet for his taste.

He went up the steps and moved behind a stack of crates. He saw a guard dressed in the green and grey CI uniform, a laser-rifle slung across his chest.

DuSalle waited until he passed, then moved along the line of crates, which ranged in all sizes, stacked high in rows. Above these was a catwalk that went diagonally from one end of the cargo area to the other. Luckily there was no one standing there. Further across was the ship that all this cargo was coming from.

He spotted Chapel who saw him and waved him over.

"What's going on, Sir?" said DuSalle. He glanced over Chapel's shoulder to Shortland and the eight Narc officers, huddled into the darkened corner between the crates.

"That, I think, is a question that only Commander Waris can answer." He gestured to a black haired woman, dressed as they all were, apart from DuSalle and Chapel, in uniform.

"Detective, where is the rest of the group?" asked the commanding officer stiffly.

"We were attacked, not sure by what, Commander," said DuSalle, sadly. "The Chief is dead. I think it was a Horizon addict, by the smell."

Waris stared at DuSalle for a moment. "Eagles should not have gone with a bunch of green Constables, but hopefully whoever attacked is out of the picture. We still need to find Eagles' contact." She looked at Chapel, Shortland and DuSalle sternly, asserting her authority. "That is still our main objective, understand?"

"Yes, ma'am," said Chapel, Shortland and DuSalle as one.

DuSalle suddenly remembered the long barrelled weapon he held in his hands. "Commander." Her head turned to him. "We may have another problem to worry about."

"And what is that, exactly?" she asked, cocking her head to the side.

DuSalle threw down the weapon in the centre of the group. "This," he said, "this is a weapon that I took from one of the criminals. He's out cold and cuffed up in the office." He looked at the assembled officers, most which were covered by caps and goggles. Both Chapel and Waris looked curiously at him. "This I believe is also a weapon that may have been used in…" he caught the warning look from Chapel. This investigation was top secret, be told to nobody. "…in a robbery attempt, and I believe there might be more stashed with the drugs."

Waris frowned. "That is a bigger problem, Detective." She nodded her thanks to DuSalle. "We've got to tread carefully with this. There are about twenty guards in this place, most were guarding the main doors where we took them out. Others will be patrolling the ship and cargo holding areas. We've got to take out the one thing that'll give us away…"

"The lights," said Chapel, nodding. "I shall do that."

"Good. Now we have to locate our contact, and arrest him," said Waris, "before he can give us away."

Chief Waris' contact was in the higher office, on top of the docking bay. DuSalle had already visited the lower office.

DuSalle, Waris and five other Narc officers waited as Chapel went off to disable the power. There was a sudden blinding flash, then darkness. Six palm beacons clicked on in unison basing the area with harsh white.

"Right," said Waris, in a hushed tone, gathering everyone around. "We have to split up. DuSalle and… Chapel, good you're back, you two go with Dempton. Shortland and Spencer, you're with me." She gestured to the remaining Narc. "You three team up. We'll meet up near to the higher office, try and avoid the guards as best you can."

Their lights were dimmed as the red emergency lighting flickered on.

"This is very strange, DuSalle," said Chapel quietly, as they moved between the dimly lit corridors walled by crates, of all sizes, stacked high in the air. "Strange indeed. Why have they got a stash of drugs and also a stash of weapons?"

"What?" DuSalle, had to stop himself from shouting. "How do you know that?" He turned to Chapel as Dempton kept watch.

"It's inside one of these crates," said Chapel, holding a crate lid in his hand. He handed it to DuSalle. "Probably many more."

"But it has an atom lock, Sir. How did you open it?"

Inspector Chapel gave DuSalle a look. "It was loose, Detective."

"But this says athletic equipment," DuSalle turned to the contents, "definitely not athletic."

"No, but these pieces, do look familiar yes?" Chapel pointed at the long barrelled weapon which DuSalle was now wielding with his Corps issue weapon holstered. The pieces embedded in foam packaging inside the crate, exactly matched the weapon he was holding.

"This is not normal behaviour for criminals, DuSalle. Two high risk finds in one place. They would not have done this by mistake." Chapel looked at the lid and pointed further down on the lid. "Here look, this crate was put here a lot earlier."

"Three months earlier, Sir!" exclaimed DuSalle, careful to keep his voice down. "Wasn't there a drop in the crime rate then, Sir?"

"Yes, there was," said Chapel, thoughtful., You know I've always believed that criminals are far more organised than the government like to think, they tend to just pass it off. But if there is a structure to the crimes here, then maybe we can lop off the head before it becomes too rested."

"You don't think that this person could be here, do you, Sir?" said DuSalle in astonishment.

"It's a minor possibility," said Chapel, replacing the lid on the crate and moving on. "If this new head criminal is here then he doesn't trust very many people."

They met up with Waris, Shortland and the others at the bottom of the metal staircase that led into a corridor. There they would find the informant by the name of Iverberg. They were just approaching one door when they heard a yell. The door burst open and guards dressed in CI uniforms poured out, roaring with laughter.

The roar of laughter turned to a roar of rage.

At this more guards poured out of other doors. They all opened fire; none of the seven shots struck the officers, but a strong whiff of ozone filled the air about them.

The three guards in front went down into a crouch as the four behind sprayed the corridor with bolts of light. They flung themselves to the ground.

Waris' weapon brought down one of the crouching guards, he tumbled backward from the impact, knocking two in the back row down with him.

DuSalle felt his arm being tugged. Before he could react, he was pulled aside. A laser bolt smashed into the wall where his head had just vacated.

"Thank you, Sir," he said gratefully. Chapel merely nodded.

"Look!" shouted Chapel suddenly, pointing behind the guards.

DuSalle turned his head to look in that direction. He saw a swirl of red hair and a booted foot disappear into a room as more guards appeared and began firing on them. They were now heavily outnumbered.

DuSalle was pulled to the side and Chapel, shouting over the weapon's fire, said, "If that's where Waris's contact is, I suspect he has passed beyond questioning. We've got to get to that ship. Stop it taking off."

Chapel shouted at Waris, explaining his plan. As she took down two guards, she nodded her assent. DuSalle and Chapel dove into the empty room, pulling off the loose vent cover and crawling through.

"DuSalle," said Chapel, as they were crawling on hands and knees in the vent, his voice echoing, "get to that ship before it takes off."

"Will do." DuSalle was just about to go when he turned back to Chapel. "What are you going to do, Sir?"

"I'm going to find the master criminal," he replied, calmly. "I saw his face, but I need to catch him in the act. If I don't, then we may never catch him."

They came to an intersection. Chapel took the right, and DuSalle took the left, toward the sounds of the main hanger.

DuSalle got out at the other end. For a moment he thought he saw movement at the front of the ship but dismissed it. The robots were still unloading the ship's cargo.

DuSalle would have to tread carefully now.

The Detective moved along a line of unpacked crates, some of which the robots were unloading onto a conveyer up to the cargo holding area.

He turned to go up the gangplank.

"You there," said a voice.

"Halt!" said another.

DuSalle turned slowly, the weapon still in his hands. "What are you doing here?"

Their weapons were trained on him. Survival had been one of DuSalle's traits thus far, but that seemed to be ebbing away.

Hoping the ruse would hold for a few seconds, he continued. "I was just looking for you." He shot the first guard in the face. He jumped behind a stack of crates to avoid the second guard.

Other shots rang out, then all was silent.

DuSalle stood up very slowly, his weapon at the ready.

He found himself looking at the remains of the Narc unit and Shortland.

"Hello, Chief, Sergeant," he said. "Thanks for the save."

"You owe us one, DuSalle," said Shortland, grinning.

"Any time, Detective," said Waris, saluting. "Now we must get…"

Suddenly a bloody fist punched through her chest and opened.

It was holding her heart.

XXVII

DuSalle turned a corner and stopped running, narrowly missing being seen by a small group of guards who marched by.

"Thought you could get away, huh, soldier boy?" He spun around to see the shadow, huge and lumbering, completely covered in blood, its and other people's, its eyes glowing ghoulishly in the darkness of its flinty face.

DuSalle brought his weapon to bare, but a large hand whipped out and almost broke his wrist. The long barrelled laser was flung aside.

He pulled out his stun-truncheon, but before he could do anything with it, it was taken from him and snapped in half, the pieces tossed away.

The creature landed a punch to DuSalle's chest which sent him flying between the crates.

He crashed through a half open door, finding himself in a small dimly lit room. Bodies were slumped against the wall, they were men and women, all with sunken faces, thin to the point of starving.

At his entrance, their eyes opened weakly.

Green-within-green eyes, frowns of weak anger on their pitiful grey faces. "Giv' us," said one, feebly, "give us hozzie."

"What?" answered DuSalle, his hand throbbing as he picked himself up.

"Give us hozzie! Hozzie now!" said another, eyes bleary and watery, leaving pale tracks over pinched features.

The door was battered away. The figure stood in the entrance and laughed.

"No Hozzie for Mozzie! No, no!" it chided.

The green-within-green eyes fled into nothingness. The thin bodies slumped down and were out again.

"Come here, soldier boy!" growled the creature hotly.

The Detective ran full pelt at the creature.

He jumped.

The creature grabbed him around the waist in mid-air and flung him sideways.

DuSalle smashed into the crates over the far side of the docking bay, spilling their contents all around him and over the floor.

Winded, DuSalle tried to sit up. Heavy footsteps told him the creature was coming. He grabbed wildly for something to throw at the creature to stop its advance. His fingers grabbed onto something and just as he was about to throw it, his full senses caught up with what he was holding.

Turning the long barrelled weapon around, he aimed at the creature, which was now building to a run.

He fired.

The area was filled with a golden radiance. For DuSalle time seemed to slow. The blood drenched monster continued to advance. Its grisly face coated in the blood of its victims. DuSalle recognised another of Poper's associates in that grime glare.

But recognition turned to shock as the weapon hummed in his hand, and all at once a bright yellow cord seemed to connect from the tip of the barrel to the heavily muscled chest of the creature.

The figure's chest exploded. The world sped up again as the head was sawn clean off, the body kept running a few paces before tripping over itself and then tumbling to a stop.

It was only then, when the head of his attacker rolled out of the blackness into a dim light, that DuSalle realised it had been a human after him.

It was Poper's Chauffeur, Yates.

A leer was still on his bald, flinty face, the eyes glinting menacingly under brushy eyebrows.

Suddenly, the ship's engines began to rumble.

* * *

DuSalle was up and running to the back of the ship. Suddenly laser bolts began to fly about him; he dove over a low pile of crates.

The Detective stood up and discharged the bright energy beam in the direction the shots had come from. The weapon destroyed most of the crates. The guards it seemed would not be continuing fire.

He turned at a noise weapon trained to see all that was left of the Narc unit.

"Hey, Detective, don't shoot us, Sir," said Dempton as three of them came out of cover.

"What's going on, Sir?" Spencer limped forward.

"What's up? Where's Chapel?" Shortland lowered her *PummelFist*.

"The Inspector has given me orders," said DuSalle. "He's got his own mission. Glad you're here," he told them with great relief, an idea suddenly forming in his mind, as the engines rose to a scream. "Here's the plan –"

He finished explaining his idea. The two nodded and went off in opposite directions. Shortland took up position beside him.

'*... get to that ship. Stop it taking off,*' Chapel had said, and that was what he was going to do.

Taking a deep breath, DuSalle and Shortland stepped out of cover.

A guard sprung out of hiding and was cut down by a sudden cross fire of laser bolts from the hidden Narc officers.

DuSalle and Shortland ran through two tall stacks of crates. The *Silver Frame* was in sight.

The entrance to the ship was at the front under the cockpit, with the massive engine housings at the back. The open cargo port was in between. The engines were whining, hot air rippling through DuSalle's hair.

"What we gonna do now, newbie?" shouted Shortland as the noise became deafening.

DuSalle looked at the massive clamps on the folded wings of the craft. Plucking his radio from his belt, he shouted, "Sir, this is DuSalle, am at the ship! It's not going anywhere."

"Is that the engine I can hear?" came Chapel's voice thinly through the wind.

"Yes, sir!" shouted DuSalle.

"And you're using the radio, DuSalle!" came Chapel's muffled voice. "The jamming field is down, which means the control systems are being hacked. The ship can bust of here at any time!"

"What? But, Sir, this is not air-sealed!"

"Exactly, Detective! You have to stop it!"

"Right." DuSalle looked at Shortland as a shadow lunged from behind the crates.

"Cargo 'bot! Gone berserk!" yelled Shortland, as the thin lumbering 'bot stretched out its long clamping arms toward them.

"Get to the front of the ship!" said DuSalle, aiming the weapon at the 'bot. "See if you can get to the pilot!"

"Right! Come on you big lug! Follow me! Come on!" she shouted at the 'bot, firing at its lamp like eyes as she ran into the crates.

The thrusters were beginning to burn red. The high-pitched scream was nearing an unbearable level, the crates were buckling and crashing around DuSalle.

DuSalle stood stock still, his arms numb, his legs frozen as the crates imploded around him. He was being engulfed, confined and surrounded. His mouth ran dry at that moment, the scream of the engines changing to his hearing to be the screams of his fellow Detectives, now added to the voices of Utah, Eagles and the rest of the Narc unit.

Then a voice penetrated the noise.

"Don't let it take off, DuSalle. Do you hear me!"

The Detective looked down at the weapon in his clenched hands, he twisted it so it was flat, then he grabbed the dial on the side of the weapon, turning it to full power, overloading it.

He ran toward the *Silver Frame*, then jumped, dropping the weapon into one of the thruster funnels. The engines exploded into life, throwing him backward across the disintegrating cargo.

The Detective got to his feet and started running, shouting at anyone still living to get away.

The high-pitched scream stopped abruptly.

The ship pulled in its landing gear.

The ship exploded.

DuSalle was hit in the back of the head, something hot grazing his cheek and was bowled over.

Falling into blackness.

XXVIII

Images burned into DuSalle.

The first meeting with Inspector, his gnarled face, diseased and rotting clawing at the Drylian Kybrint, tearing off his arm. Instead of blood names, places, numbers spilled out of him, his lies, deceits and his crimes for all to see, Chapel gnawing at his severed arm with relish.

Then DuSalle was in Poper's office, but not in the office, but part of the Fellis holo' image. Poper was pushing him into the fiery pit, grinning like the devil. His face blurred and phased into Chapel's, reaching out to catch DuSalle, but he pulled away in horror.

Then he was in the entrance of Naming's flat, but instead of Shortland it was Balla standing naked over the shipmate, the stun truncheon a severed limb – Kybrint's arm, falling down on Naming's bloodied face, information pouring out.

Until at last his head came off and rolled to DuSalle's feet.

DuSalle opened his eyes, his senses screaming as they returned.

"Awake at last, Detective?" said a familiar voice from his left.

He sat up and looked around. To his amazement he found himself in the medical wing of the Eastern Quad Base.

DuSalle turned to see Chapel sat at his side.

"S – sir," he stuttered, "what happened? Where are…"

Chapel waved away the questions. "I shall tell you all that on the way, DuSalle." He stood. "Get dressed and I'll fill you in."

"Why the uniform, Sir?" asked DuSalle, looking at the Inspector. "I thought you didn't have to wear them."

DuSalle got up, slowly, as his head throbbed dully. The microwave compress on his injured thigh made him wobble to his feet, as it healed and knitted together the fracture.

The Detective managed to cover the wince as his bandaged elbow pulsed with pain as he stood up.

"In this instance," said Chapel, standing up and reaching for the door of the private room, "where we're going it will be necessary to tell people apart from the rest."

As DuSalle was left with that cryptic remark, he wondered how the Inspector had gotten his uniform. Had he been to his flat or gotten a replica from the Quad Base stores? He straightened his armour and thrust his cap into his left armpit and stepped out of the room, into the cleansed corridor. He saw the sun was murkily setting in the large window at the other end of the white corridor.

"So how long have I been out, Sir?"

"Don't worry you haven't missed the main event," said Chapel, as they took the Inspector's patrol car out on to the streets. He noticed that Chapel, who was driving, was favouring his left hand. "Though I do have news for you."

"Yes, Sir?" asked DuSalle, eagerly.

"Councillor Balla is dead," said the Inspector simply, turning off the main sky way.

DuSalle was dumbstruck for a moment, then, as his throat was devoid of any moisture at all, "How, Sir?"

"The Constable killed her," said Chapel, still looking intently forward. "It was confirmed by forensics, blood was in her mouth and on her face. Security monitors had been tampered with, but that was enough evidence to go on."

"I thought it was Cartier doing this," said DuSalle, a sense of loss within him, he tried to displace it. "He's dead, who took over?"

"Who indeed, Detective," said Chapel, looking at him for the first time. "Whose mess were they really cleaning up, hers or Cloves?"

"You mean it was either the Isolationists or this assassin?"

"Doesn't fit either MO, does it, DuSalle?" said Chapel. "But the Constable has been brainwashed in some way. If only I could find her. There was a pattern, I was close to it. I was almost sure."

"What changed, Sir?"

"Several things," said Chapel, looking back at the traffic. DuSalle noticed how familiar the skies were getting to him. "First this move on one of their own. The PIM have only gone for buildings that were empty of life, places that were under construction, now they have targeted people, raided from files that Clove was handling in Balla's presence."

"So all their information was from her? Against her will?" asked DuSalle, amazed.

"They had the inside track on us, DuSalle, and no one knew, not even Balla with her shifting loyalties."

"Which didn't sit well with the extremists," said DuSalle, thinking of Balla in his flat, her face bright and craving.

"Exactly. They discovered Clove and his dealings with the Benefactor, but I don't believe they stopped him."

"There was a report the Constable filed," said DuSalle, remembering the files that Chapel had shown him. "A magistrate, unnamed at the time, had been attacked by a street gang; no arrests were filed."

"Right outside *La Flayed Dragon*, as I recall. It plays a part in this all, DuSalle," said Chapel, grimly. "That's why Cartier was going to blow it up and us along with it, to keep the Constable safe, though she has not been tracked so far."

"Cartier was bringing it up a notch, Sir," said DuSalle. "He knew something was going on, feeling he had no voice he would make a violent statement."

"Precisely, Detective. Consumed as he was by the death of his sister, the IJ didn't catch onto him and his activities. They probably financed his whole operation through his admin contacts in various Sections of the Security Corps, I shouldn't wonder."

Chapel changed lanes and moved into the shadow of a stately looking Stakk-Flat. "There is another rub to this, however, DuSalle. Poper."

"How so, Sir?"

"Clove was an envoy for the Stellar Sovereignty, but he was shipped in with Poper and his team. Quite a big deal for Cobble Industries," said Chapel. "Though they have big contracts with the Stels and Regs, Cobble Industries and Poper are independent and all-encompassing of politicking and such, their cargo of weapons…"

"But, Sir, surely as witnesses to this as we are, we could forward our statements of the night in the docking bay?" interjected DuSalle.

"My reputation precedes me, DuSalle," said Chapel, bitterly. "Were it not for form and rank, I would be tossed aside into ruin. My word is without clout, as would yours be, and that of Shortland. Proof is the only way, otherwise it is my own supposed myopic vision on a criminal state within Chandler City and the galaxy itself." The Inspector sighed heavily. "Poper is behind it, I am sure, but nothing I have will ever stick. He is made on this planet, in this city, DuSalle." Chapel shrugged. "I may not be able to cut off his hold here, but I can stop it from tightening its grip."

"So we can only deal with what we have, Sir," said DuSalle, in more of a statement. "Then there is Cartier, the death of Balla, the Constable and the assassination of Clove."

"That there is, DuSalle," agreed Chapel. "Three months into his opening negotiations with Pelimar, Clove is assassinated by a weapon from off world, thus ruling out the Isolationists who would have nothing to do with outsiders. So it leaves us with two alternatives – either the Pastoral Regions, who do not particularly like the Stellar Sovereignty though are not at this point openly at war with them, or the Sovereignty itself."

"There might be a... third party," said DuSalle, slowly.

"Oh," said Chapel, just as slowly, "and who might that be, Detective?"

"Our own government, perhaps, Sir?" said DuSalle. "The upper hierarchy of the government has been quiet about this." He raised an eyebrow.

"Hmm," said Chapel, thoughtfully. "That is a possibility. Some elements of every government can be fanatical enough to wish to murder each other to get what they want. Sad, but unfortunately true."

"But then again," said Chapel after a moment silence, "what would members of the Chamber of Patrons have to gain in that respect? We would have to deal with the Sovereignty at some point in this."

DuSalle, feeling his head about to explode with millions of wild ideas, said instead, "Tell me what happened after that explosion in the docking bay, Sir," finally voicing the thought that had been nagging him since he awoke.

"That I can do easily, DuSalle," said Chapel, recounting the events after the explosion, which caused DuSalle to knock his head and lose consciousness.

The explosion which had happened above ground had taken out the floor of the docking bay and the demolished ship and one or two guards had been plunged down on to the cargo floor, half of that being of an explosive nature, so destroying the ship further. The sole pilot of the ship was killed outright and the already dead bodies of the guards being vaporised by a second explosion that had gutted the ship and the back office, leaving no evidence.

Only seven of the original thirty guards were arrested, most of them with serious injuries or minor bruises. None of the actual smugglers were caught, the informer having been killed before the raid or any officers could question him.

Chapel had sustained injuries, but not as serious as Shortland who would be in traction for a month. Only DuSalle had been bruised and a little burnt by both explosions. The synthi-skin on his cheek still felt stiff.

"…But back to our present situation," said Chapel, "for a fact we know that a delegation is coming here from the Sovereignty…"

"What?" blurted DuSalle. "Oh, yes. Sorry, Sir, I'd forgotten."

"This delegation has in fact landed," continued Chapel. He turned off another corner. "The Isolationists had nothing to do with the assassination – that we know because the weapon used was not of a kind made here. The envoy gets a lift with Poper's lot. The docking bay was swept by Narc. Apart from the badly burnt corpses there was no other trace of Horizon."

"You mean it was just the weapon parts?"

Chapel shrugged. "That is now debatable, as no physical evidence exists of the weapons cache."

"Impossible!" blurted DuSalle.

"No, merely improbable, Detective. Nothing is impossible," said Chapel, with false cheer. "The docking bay as we speak is being cleaned up and remodelled by Poper's crew, authorised by Vice and the Benefactor. Any slim traces of weapon parts will be erased."

"What if some of it was shipped out? That we know of from the docking bay," said DuSalle.

"Exactly the point I raised but was ignored," said Chapel. "Vice was all set to get us off the case, but I was able to swing it a bit, which led us here on our present course of action."

"Where to, Sir?" asked DuSalle. He was unsure of their destination.

"Where else, DuSalle?" said Chapel, with a smile. "The Conference Dome."

XXIX

A massive opulently built configuration, the Beneficial Conference Dome was built over the very spot where the first foundations of Chandler City began.

Chapel and DuSalle were cruising toward the soaring pale arc of the Dome in the distance.

The radio chirped and DuSalle took up the handset.

"This pat seven-niner-four, reading you!" said DuSalle.

"Connection from SWT, Chief Hallow."

"Connect him, DuSalle," said Chapel, his eyes bright.

DuSalle coughed and addressed the handset.

After a moment, sounds of rattling fire were heard in the distance.

"Hello, Hallow!" said Chapel. "You have info for me?"

DuSalle stared at Chapel.

"Yes, Inspector," said Hallow, excitedly. "You have posed a quite interesting hypothesis. We were delight…"

"I am in a rush I'm afraid, Chief, this information is crucial to closing a case," said Chapel, kindly.

"Of course, Inspector," said Hallow, slightly put out. "The weapon you described would have to be very heavy duty. Radiation in such a device is key, modulation of which makes it useless otherwise. However, the device could be used over a considerable distances – the longer the distance, the less radiation burn-off from the beam."

"You mean the longer the distance the lower the radiation effect on the person using it?" said Chapel.

"Yes. The beam will be tight, it would need to be focused on a certain distance, though that is a snag!"

"How do you mean?" asked DuSalle.

"Well the beam would have to build up. It would cut through anything, but if it were to cut from a certain distance, maybe if it was programmed, the target would have heat on them," said Hallow.

"But…" said DuSalle, but Chapel cut across him.

"There would be heat, conduction on the skin of the target, then, yes?"

"Ah, well," said Hallow, "it depends on the output of the device, but the cut would be intensely tight. The heat would not be instantaneous, but rather quick."

"The subject would feel it then? Move before the charge struck true?" said Chapel looking at DuSalle.

"Well yes, they would certainly feel something," said Hallow. "The flight instinct would cut in, however, making them want to move out of the heat."

"Unless they didn't want to," said Chapel quietly.

"Sorry, Inspector, didn't catch –"

"Thank you, Chief Hallow," said Chapel, motioning DuSalle to replace the handset. "You have been very helpful."

The patrol car fell into silence again. DuSalle was aching with questions, but Chapel's rather unapproachable expression, heeded any thought of speech.

As DuSalle was looking around, his thoughts turned to what they were to do upon crashing this important party. He noticed another patrol car behind them.

"Sir, I think…"

"I see them, Detective!" exclaimed Chapel.

Chapel brought his patrol car down by the large multi-layered gravic fountain, a monument to the planet's achievement in gravity manipulation. Chapel and DuSalle jumped out as the patrol car behind them closed.

As they ran toward the sloping steps, the patrol car zoomed in front of them, swerving to a stop.

DuSalle recognised the markings as Brig and Wayne exited the vehicle.

"Sergeant Brig, Constable Wayne! How nice to see both!" greeted Chapel cheerily.

"Hold it!" hissed Brig, raising his *PummelFist*, "Vice has ordered your immediate detainment, Chapel. You are off the case. We have reason to believe the Constable is here to commit murder!"

"Then let us pass!" said DuSalle, squaring up to the tall Wayne. "Let's end it here!"

"We have orders to detain you," said Wayne, silkily, "not about protecting you."

"More people to die for you, Chapel?" spat Brig. "I don't think so."

"Even more will die unless you let us past, Sergeant!" shouted Chapel. "You will do as I order!"

"We do as the Chief orders, unlike you…" Chapel's vicious upper cut caught Brig by surprise, downing him at once.

DuSalle had to grapple with Wayne who was stronger, but DuSalle was carrying his stun-truncheon.

With three quick jabs and a punch in the stomach, the Sergeant was sprawled. Using their handcuffs, Brig and Wayne were attached to the door handles of their patrol vehicle, their weapons tossed and locked inside their patrol car, out of their reach when they awoke.

"Come on, DuSalle," said Chapel, turning toward the door. "We have no time to waste now!"

They entered and ran past the unmanned reception desk. They came up to a fork in the well carpeted corridor, the one on the left leading up to the stairs to the observatory for the press, the barrier of which had been broken, the other on the right led to the conference hall itself.

DuSalle knew that the observatory for the press would not be in use. This was a top-secret meeting, after all.

"DuSalle, go to the conference and tell them to get out," said Chapel as both he and DuSalle drew their weapons. "I'll try and talk the assassin out of this."

"Are you sure you can?" asked DuSalle, eyebrows raised.

"I can at least try," said Chapel with a grim smile. "Now go!"

DuSalle went down the right-hand corridor, seeing Chapel move up the left. He ran down the winding corridor, feeling sweat break out on his forehead. His leg began to ache as he burst through the double doors into the conference room.

If you could call it a room; it was more a large domed chamber, with hundreds of tiers of seats, decked out like the first level of a hov-ball stadium, with the central Speaker's Table in the middle headed by the Mediator's Chair, set on a dais so that anyone sat on the chair could look over the table and most of the assembled patrons.

Those assembled around it hadn't seemed to have noticed him. There were twelve of them sat in equal groups either side of the table. DuSalle recognised only one of them: at the head of the six on the left was the Benefactor of Chandler City, so that meant that on the right, with three guards were the Stellar Sovereignty delegates. One of them looked in DuSalle's direction.

"Quickly, sir," DuSalle shouted to the Benefactor who swung around in his seat, "we have to…."

"*ASSASIN*!" screamed the lead delegate who looked past the Benefactor straight at DuSalle. He looked somewhat familiar to DuSalle, but before the Detective could place him the three Sovereignty guards lunged at him.

Bringing him to the ground, the Detective was slammed backwards and was turned over on his front, a knee in his back and his arms twisted behind him.

The double doors suddenly burst open again and a Security Corps officer stepped in.

So Chapel *had* called in back up. DuSalle was relieved, at least he didn't have to deal with this on his own, at least he...

The woman officer pulled her weapon out of her holster and pointed it straight at the Sovereignty delegation, gliding quickly to the bottom of the steps, just above DuSalle. "Independence to Pelimar!" hissed the woman officer through a strangely wide grin.

It all happened very quickly.

The woman continued to descend the steps towards the Sovereignty delegation. DuSalle struggled with the shocked guards and tried to point his weapon at the woman.

Suddenly a window above collapsed into jagged shards as two figures crashed out of the observation lounge above.

A fiery golden line exploded from between the falling figures, striking the ground around the Constable and ripping her apart. A mess of flesh and blood slithered to the floor with the two still writhing figures dropping into it, showered in stars of sparkling glass.

The figure that had fallen under the first kicked him in the stomach, throwing him off.

The man on the floor was Chapel, covered in the gory mess of what had been a woman five seconds earlier.

The other man, regaining his balance, stood and lunged at Chapel. DuSalle saw the glint of a knife, he wasted no more time.

He aimed. He fired.

The black-covered figure had gained a hole in his belly. After what seemed an eternity as the man stood there, he finally fell sideways, sprawling over the seats normally occupied by the Beneficial government of Chandler City.

Chapel stood and brushed the tiny shards of glass and gristle off his now blood-stained uniform.

"Very nice shot, DuSalle," said Chapel with a smile. He turned to the stunned assembly. "Now I think you all need to hear this…"

"What the hell is going on?" burst out one of the Sovereignty delegates.

"Let me explain, first," said Chapel, holding up a finger. "The investigation we were put on at the start of this was the assassination of one Tyler Clove, an envoy for the Stellar Sovereignty, who you had sent ahead to put in motion this very meeting. He had been killed by an unknown assailant who most assumed were the Isolationists of this planet. In fact Clove has not only died once." Chapel bent down and removed the mask from the dead assassin. "But twice."

Tyler Clove's green eyes stared blankly at the high domed ceiling.

XXX

The sight shocked the Stellar Sovereignty delegates and the Benefactor and his assistants but most of all, DuSalle.

"I suggest," said Chapel, holding up a finger. DuSalle got to his feet along with Chapel, the delegates still staring shocked at the black-clad figure on the floor. "That you all listen to what I have to say." He coughed and then said, "But I forget my manners. My name is Inspector Jason Chapel of the Security Corps of Chandler City." He clicked his booted heels and saluted at the Benefactor. "Your plan was very cleverly laid out, I'll give you that." He smiled at the Sovereignty delegates. "A good set-up, without the need of the biggest effort on your part, if only you had done your research on this planet a little better…"

"What you talking about?" sputtered the head of the delegates angrily.

"I'm talking about the fact, Arch General Gains," he nodded to the head delegate, who had been the one to cry assassin at DuSalle's arrival in the chamber, "that you tried to blame someone else for your little trick, namely this government." He looked pointedly at the Benefactor, then continued. "Killing one of your own people, or at least a clone of one of your own, then go to the galactic media and blame us for the his death, where the trust between the two peoples would collapse, moving you to place a military garrison here in punishment, which would have been helped considerably by a second death of a higher ranking and suitably more notable figure." He gestured toward the Arch General who was now fuming. "Martyrdom from a war hero of such stature within the Stellar Sovereignty would have sealed this planet's fate, yes? While the assassin of both Sovereignty citizens would go into hiding to await the arrival of the invasion force."

The lead delegate of the Sovereignty's looked at Chapel. With a slight snigger he said, "Invasion? Is this what you believe?"

"Indeed, Sir, very clever. But for two things." Chapel picked up the long thin blade with a grim smile. "The weapon used on Clove was not of Chandler City make and trying to blame the Isolationists for this attack failed. Isolationists hate anything and everything from the outside. The second thing was what Clove and you failed to take into account of was how he arrived here. He hitched a lift with Cobble Industries. I had the flight plan of the ship, a ship which was almost totally destroyed in the docking bay explosions. Recovering and studying them I made a few off world inquiries… yes Arch General, you may well raise your eyebrows at that… and discovered that there was a compartment large enough to place a man into it – having one man doing the writ and law in unison with Pelimar while the clone hid up for a while, but the man – sorry men," the Inspector smiled at the Benefactor, "had vices both useful and unforeseen. Is that not right, Arch General?" He looked at the Arch General hard. "As they are clones of you, you should know how chaotic they would be – how unbidden and bountiful they would be."

"Nonsense, they could not be more unlike me!" stated Gains viciously.

"Pah!" tutted Chapel. "You can see it, Benefactor. All of you, that they bear a resemblance!" He turned on the Arch General again. "Clove seduced Balla, enabling him not only to bring the government into line, as she had the ear of the Benefactor, but also allowing him to meet and greet with the criminal classes in the bed of Constable Warren." He tipped his head sadly at the remains of the poor Constable. "Horizon to be shipped back to the Stellar Sovereignty, in Clove's body," he turned to The Arch General, "while the new weapons are shipped to the Pastoral Regions."

"What?" barked the Benefactor, speaking for the first time.

"Preposterous nonsense!" said Arch General Gains. "I've heard of you; you see conspiracy all about you, perhaps you killed him, eh? Maybe you are to blame!"

"Oh yes," said Chapel continued. "I get that a lot, but consider this. The Arch General is of the mind that is shared in the higher ranks of the Dynasts of The Sovereignty – the war is ending. The Feuds are finished. What better way to jump start a new campaign?" Chapel looked around the delegates. "With a new player, of course! But they needed a patsy for the media, a stronger influence than anyone in this room will admit, to believe it. So kill Clove, see that the Pastoral Regions have weapons to fight, while troops are loaded with the new Horizon drug, and Pelimar is destroyed in the mix; all very tragic! Yes?"

"Of course not!" growled the Arch General. "Benefactor, please…"

"You wish to use us in service of another war, Arch General, but it is not of our doing."

"That's it, Inspector?" said Arch General Gains. "You think that is our great plan?" He cast his eyes over the body of the clone and DuSalle and the Benefactor. "You think it's that easy, that simple to create a war, do you? Think all there is to it, do you, Inspector? I have led thousands of campaigns into the furthest reaches of the galaxy, destroyed continents, sacked worlds, and detonated stars. Think I would suffer to enlist this planet for war?"

"Think?" said Chapel, with a smile at the Benefactor, who was now glaring at the Sovereignty delegates. "I know."

"Prove it!" growled the head delegate. "Go on, prove it!"

"Oh, but I can't," said Chapel, "both Cloves are dead, but if I were to check his DNA against the files I have obtained 'under the counter', shall we say. I could very well prove that Clove is not Clove," he continued with a thin smile, "but you Arch General. Martyrdom twice." He looked at the clone. "No, thrice over. Who would know what he is truly capable of more than yourself?" Chapel smiled. "Also, if this information was leaked to the substantially protected media of the Stellar Sovereignty, your people would be extremely displeased with the governorships trying to lord over a small and barely defendable planet, wouldn't they?"

The delegate glared at Chapel, but it was different from the one he had begun with; it was a glare of defeat, and if DuSalle could see it then so could Chapel, and more importantly, so could the Benefactor.

"Thank you for your time, Sir," said Chapel, bowing low to the Benefactor.

The delegates of the Stellar Sovereignty were arrested on the spot and were ushered out by the Benefactor's own guard, who had disarmed the Sovereignty guards. They were taken away to the ship, loaded with the bodies of both cloves and were to be escorted out of the restriction zone around the planet.

The Benefactor sat now in one of the Conference Dome's chairs. The rest of the place was swarming with medics and officers, tidying up the scene so that the reporters wouldn't guess there had been an incident here.

"Now this assassination is cleared up," said Chief Vice, who had appeared on the scene, looking around as the various officers cleared up the mess, "what about that officer?"

"She was the missing Constable I was investigating before all of this." A small smile appeared on his face. "I was nearly at the end of the case, and would have easily finished it apart from Clove's death stopping me, but I took up the case again…"

"I thought I assigned you to off *this* case?" said Chief Vice, looking annoyed.

"You did, Sir," said Chapel, still with a small smile. "As I was ordered, after that docking explosion, but I get ahead of myself."

"Well?" said Vice impatiently.

"The young constable had in fact been kidnapped and brainwashed, and has left a considerable amount of damage behind her," said Chapel, looking grave. "Ordered around like a puppet on a string by a group of fanatical isolationists."

"The People's Island did this?"

"I'm afraid so, Sir," said Chapel. "Ben Kelly was the suspected leader of that group, one of the reasons it is so well known. But his group didn't know about the envoy or his assassination; it was someone else."

"That's true, Sir," said DuSalle. "Cartier knew about the assassination through Balla's files. He didn't want us to pin it on Kelly."

"Cartier knew we were working on a big case," said Chapel. "Rumour is easily spread, so he had us followed so that he could find out what we knew. Out of impatience or pride, he attacked."

"You said this Constable was brainwashed to do the Isolationist's bidding?" said Chief Vice, trying to get on track.

"Yes, Sir, I did," said Chapel. "She was actually responsible for the Stel murders and that of Councillor Balla."

"You understand," said Chief Vice, as they moved toward the Benefactor slumped in his chair, "that none of what was said or done here goes beyond this room."

"Understood, Sir," said Chapel, he held up a hand. "Perhaps I can ask a question of you, Sir?"

"Yes," said the Benefactor, his usually smooth features crinkled.

"I want to keep DuSalle here on as my partner," said Chapel, a slight smile curling his lips once again. "That way we can make sure that we don't let anything slip."

"Are you threat…"

"I would like also," Chapel continued, "for DuSalle to be rewarded for his sterling services to the city. You can make up any story you wish, of course," he added.

"You said," gritted the Benefactor, "that you wanted to ask a question."

"Yes," said Chapel, "and it is this. Why were you going against the whim of the city to become part of the Stellar Sovereignty?"

The Benefactor studied Chapel's thin face for a moment.

"This city is beginning to grow in on itself, almost two billion residents, Inspector." The Benefactor rose up, sitting straighter in his seat. "They are rebounding off the walls, fighting and clawing at each other. They have a great need for renewal; we are a city that is on the verge of stagnating, collapsing into ourselves."

"Then why the Stellar Sovereignty?" asked Chapel, cocking an eyebrow.

"As you know, Inspector," said the Benefactor, "we were originally part of a interplanetary federation, a stable government system, which we lost contact with ten centuries ago. Now we have been independent for almost all of that time, we have adapted well, the time has come to be part of it all again, yet we are still unstable."

"Now, you believe times must change," said Chapel, nodding his head slightly.

"I do, yes," said the Benefactor. "I have decided that this city must move forward and be more of a part of the wider galaxy, to inhabit and see outside these glass domes and these hemmed-in walls."

"But why the Sovereignty?' asked Chapel again.

"I and many of my assistants have done considerable work on the matter, Inspector," said Benefactor, "and we have found that they share similar problems to our own."

"Surely then, Sir," said Chapel, "that is an awful thing to fall in with the Stellar Sovereignty."

"What? Why?" the Benefactor burst out.

"Because, Sir," said Chapel, calmly, "if they have the same problems as we do, it doesn't mean that they will cancel out the problem if we work together. It fact it raises more problems than it solves."

"Such as?"

"Such as,'" repeated Chapel, then after a pause, "their laws and rules are much different to the ones we set up. The way they act is completely different to the way we do things. It will clash all the way down the line."

"But I have decided to…" began the Benefactor.

"That is just it, Sir," said Chapel. "You may have decided, but what about the people in your city? Have you bothered to ask them what they want to do for the future of this city?"

"I was going to lead up to it, Inspector," said the Benefactor, his resolute features crumbling somewhat, "but events today do show me that I should speak up now before it completely gets out of hand."

"I see. Thank you, Sir."

XXXI

The sun fell on the horizon of Chandler City's cityscape. As they left the Conference Dome, they drove along the expressway into the corporate area of the city.

"So what now, sir?" asked DuSalle.

"Now we complete our business, DuSalle," said Chapel.

They came up to the CI building, still dwarfed by the buildings either side of it, but seeming more shadowy and sinister in the stark light.

Taking an ascend shaft, as they took the more public entrance, rather than the air stands, they walked up several corridors, past the secretary's empty desk and into Poper's office.

Sat at the desk framed by a wall of glass that pictured the thin glow of the Pelimarian sun against two high buildings was Simon Poper dressed in a grey pinstripe executive suit, dark hair slicked back against his skull.

His secretary Kathryn Pierce, was scratching notes onto a paid with her holo'stylus.

If it wasn't for the change in clothing, DuSalle would have thought it was a few days ago rather than now.

The Managing President of Cobble Industries and its various subsidiaries looked up from his work; a faint smile spread on his lips, as Chapel and DuSalle descended on him.

"What can I do for you today, officers?" said Poper.

"Simply this," said Chapel, his voice unusually stern. He pointed a finger at Poper. "I know that you were at Docking

Bay 46 on the night of the docking bay explosion." Poper looked impassive. "You can deny it, but I know what I saw and I'll be watching you closely from now on, Mr. Poper."

"What proof do you have exactly, Inspector?" said Poper. He was not smiling, but DuSalle felt the amusement in his voice in his manner toward them.

"None so far."

"Then you…"

"Kathryn, please," Poper held up his hand, "I have suffered fatal losses within my authority, Inspector. My chauffeur and my doctor are dead. Many of my guards, who were unexpectedly present, were killed. I have sent condolences to their families."

"What about Naming and his activities?" said DuSalle, staring hard Poper, who smiled.

"I cannot monitor my entire workforce, Constable. Forgive me, Detective," said Poper. "Naming has admitted his dealings with Clove. I was unaware of this; he is to be punished by your letter of the law, is he not?"

"Yes, that he is," Chapel leaned forward. "I have yet to find something against you, but be assured, I will, Mr. Poper."

"Very well, Inspector Chapel," said Poper, the smile back on his lips, "but you'll find evidence of criminal doings hard to obtain against me."

DuSalle glared at Poper angrily and was about to say something, but Chapel stopped him. "As long as we understand each other, Poper-san, Pierce-san," he said.

Chapel bowed low, his eyes never leaving Poper. The Inspector and the Detective strode out.

"So that's it then, Sir," said DuSalle, as they went through the corridors of the building. "Case closed?"

"Oh, yes, Detective," said the Inspector. "Case closed, until the next one, of course."

"What do you mean, Sir?"

"You believe this is it, Detective?" said Chapel. "That the criminals will hunker down and fade, that the Sovereignty will retreat with their tail between their legs and never bother us again?"

"Well, you did trounce them, Sir," said DuSalle, with a small grin.

"I may have stalled them, Detective," said the Inspector, "but I have not stopped them. Arch General Gains will go back in shame, possibly plot revenge against me or the Security Corps or the Benefactor and this city. Possibly his shame will cause him to leave this material world and end his life, or it will be ended for him, for his failure."

"But we're not against the Stellar Sovereignty!" exclaimed DuSalle as they made their way into the foyer.

"Not how they will see it, DuSalle," said Chapel, frowning. "We have gained an enemy, but one that will have to be slyer and cleverer in future. Then, of course, we have Poper, I have slackened his grip, but he still has a hold." Chapel shook his head disgustedly.

"Then of course there are the Isolationists, Sir," said the Detective.

"Yes, the Constable's string pullers," Chapel smiled grimly. "Yes that is our task, Detective, certainly."

DuSalle and Chapel lapsed in silence as they exited the CI building.

"Sir," said DuSalle, "why would people object to joining a bigger government than this one?"

"Because, DuSalle," said Chapel, "people are too stuck to their ideals."

"What's that got to do with…"

"People are chained to their lives, Detective, their jobs and beliefs," said Chapel. "Most can't be shaken from their chains, sometimes they gain new links or new chains altogether, but with difficulty. Some are so chained to their beliefs, they believe in a better world before this. Stupid of course, but that is a chain some like cling to, like Cartier did."

"And like Brig and Wayne," said DuSalle.

"Yes. They cling to law which should have been changed a month after they voted it into effect," said Chapel. "Links to the past bind us so strongly for all the wrong reasons, once the original reasons have faded."

"Do you think we can form..." DuSalle smiled and then continued, "forge new chains with the outside, Sir, like we had centuries ago?"

"I don't know," said Chapel equally, with a smile. "For this is the chained city, DuSalle. Someday, I am sure those chains *will* be broken."